A VALENTINE'S DAY GIFT

KYLIE GILMORE

Cover design by Sweet 'N Spicy Designs

Published by: Extra Fancy Books

ISBN-13: 978-1-942238-62-1

Where it all began…

1

Allie Marino found herself tearing up over the happy chaos of their Sunday family dinner. Her fully grown children—three sons and three stepsons—valued this weekly time together as much as she and her husband, Vinny, did. Her sons rarely missed a dinner, and now they were so blessed to have six daughters-in-law, two seven-month-old granddaughters, and a three-year-old grandson.

She exchanged a look with Vinny sitting at the head of the table next to her. His dark eyes warmed on hers. He was just as happy as she was to have this special time together. They were in the large Victorian in Clover Park, where their family began, only now it was her oldest son, Gabe's house. Her Marino stepsons were dark-haired, olive-skinned Italians like their dad—Vince, Nico, and Angel—bonded like true brothers to her light-haired, fair-skinned sons—Gabe, Luke, and Jared. Not an easy path to bonding, but they got there eventually.

Her youngest stepson, Angel, with his dark brown tousled hair and dimpled smile, looked over at her and then Vinny. "Julia and I wanted to talk to you guys."

Allie grabbed Vinny's hand under the table in anxious excitement. Angel and Julia were newlyweds and had been open about starting a family. "Is Julia pregnant?" Her voice came out so loud the entire table quieted. Even her granddaughters stopped babbling.

"No," Angel said.

"Sorry," Julia said, pushing her long dark brown hair behind her ears. "We didn't mean to get your hopes up. We're hoping soon."

Allie worked hard to hide her disappointment. "Is everything okay?"

"Yes," Julia said with a smile. "We were planning on surprising you with a keepsake book of photos and memories leading up to your wedding because you've been so supportive of all of us with our weddings. Cat's out of the bag now, I guess. We couldn't do it because no one had any pictures."

"And only you two have the memories," Angel added.

Allie tensed. Their relationship was not something she was willing to share with the kids. No sense digging around in the past.

"Do you two have any pictures from when you were dating?" Julia asked.

Allie turned to Vinny, hoping he'd shut down this whole line of questioning, but he merely shrugged one bulky shoulder. She didn't want to sound like she was hiding a secret, but it was hard for her to outright lie. The way things had unfolded between her and Vinny might be seen, in the wrong context, as scandalous. Better not to open that can of worms at all.

She turned back to Angel and Julia. "I don't think we do."

"Not everybody had a camera in their pocket like they do now," Vinny said.

Allie glanced down the table at Gabe, who was staring at his plate, not eating. Gabe knew. He was the one who'd found the letters in her old art studio. He'd read at least one that she knew about, and had confronted Vinny about it. Vinny had gotten defensive, which probably told Gabe all he needed to know.

"Any special memories from back then?" Julia asked.

"Not much to tell," Vinny said with a note of finality. "We

met, we dated, we got married, same as most couples. End of story."

Yes. Some things were private.

~

Back when it all began...

Allie Reynolds hurried to answer the front door. The construction crew for her new art studio must be here. She could hardly believe it was really happening. Her husband, William, had always considered her art to be a frivolous hobby. They'd compromised on the art studio by having it made into a full studio apartment with galley kitchen and bathroom. She had no problem with the added amenities even if it was because, as he said, "at least they could get some rental income when she finally moved on to more important endeavors." There was no love between her and her husband, an uptight workaholic lawyer. They'd married in a hurry when she got pregnant with her oldest son, and she'd been paying the price for her impulsive decision ever since. Not that William noticed she was unhappy, or noticed her at all, really. If it weren't for her three boys, the light of her life, she would've left him long ago. But the boys were all in school now and, for the first time in years, she had her mornings to herself, which meant art time.

She opened the door to two men wearing blue T-shirts that read Marino and Sons Construction, along with worn jeans and work boots. The older man, thirtysomething, definitely Italian, made a strong commanding impression between his massive size—over six feet tall and bulky with muscles—to his serious expression. She figured he was the one in charge. The younger man, early twenties, was thin and wiry and stood a little behind his boss.

The large man spoke in a deep melodious voice that had her leaning in. "I'm Vinny Marino. We're here to work on your garage." Their eyes met, and her breath caught at the incredible sadness in his dark brown eyes framed with thick lashes. It was like looking in a mirror—the joy sucked out of him just like her. He was strikingly handsome otherwise with thick dark brown hair, chiseled cheekbones, strong jaw, and full sensuous lips. If he smiled, he would no doubt be stunning, but he didn't smile.

Vinny spoke again. "It's the detached garage over there, right?" He gestured over to it.

She snapped to attention. "Yes. I'll get the key. Sorry." She turned to get it and then stopped. "I'm Allison."

Vinny nodded. "Nice to meet you, Allison. This is Tony."

Tony lifted a hand in greeting.

She grabbed the key from the kitchen hook and joined them outside. They walked over to the garage together. Vinny kept pace with her, Tony trailing behind. She was a petite five feet three, but next to Vinny, she felt tiny. Her head came up to his huge bicep, his shoulders were massive, his neck thick. She'd bet he used to play football. His stride was slow and easy, and she realized he'd deliberately slowed down to match her shorter steps. Her husband always strode ahead of her, leaving her behind with the kids.

"We're using the garage more like a shed right now," she said. "There's an access panel to get upstairs. It's basically just storage on the second level, but the roof is high enough you can stand up."

"So you're looking for it to be a rental?" Vinny asked.

"Actually, it's going to be my art studio," she confided.

"You're an artist?" Vinny asked.

She suddenly wanted to own it, to declare her real passion in life despite the fact that no one had ever bought one of her creations. "Yes. I paint."

"Very cool," Vinny said.

Warmth stole through her. His casual comment meant so much to her. "I love it," she confessed.

Vinny inclined his head. "That explains the oversized windows. You want lots of light."

"Yes." They reached the two-car detached garage and she unlocked it, opening one of the bays. It was packed full of stuff—lawn mower, shovels, rakes, the boys' old crib, assorted boxes piled up. She belatedly realized she should've cleared it out, though some of the pieces were too heavy for her to manage on her own. Her boys—Gabe, Luke, and Jared —weren't old enough to help much at eleven, seven, and five respectively. Her husband probably would've blown it off, saying he had to catch up on paperwork. Even when he was home, it wasn't like he was really home.

She turned to the men. "I'm sorry. We should've cleared this out for you."

"No problem," Vinny said. "We'll clear a path. Just show me where the access panel is."

She squeezed in between rows of crap to the center of the space and pointed up.

Vinny smiled a little, the smile not reaching his sad brown eyes. "Thanks, Allison. We'll take it from here."

She nodded and got out of their way.

Vinny moved like he had lead in his limbs, but he had to work. He had mouths to feed. The small job converting a storage space to a studio apartment was ideal for his barely functioning state. He was sure that was why his dad, the owner of Marino and Sons Construction, had given it to him, knowing he couldn't handle anything more complex while Vinny grieved his wife. Maria had died a little over a month ago after a long painful struggle with ovarian cancer. She was the love of his life, his high school sweetheart. They hadn't married right away. She'd wanted to go to college, so he'd waited. She was book smart, in love with literature and poetry, beautiful inside and out. He was "hands-on smart," as she always said. Sometimes he wondered why she didn't just find some college guy more like her, but she loved him, and he loved her more than anything in the world. They married right after she graduated college. Vince Jr. was born four years later, Nico came along two years after that, and then two years later they had Angelo.

His boys, now nine, seven, and five, were in mourning just

like him. He worried especially over five-year-old Angelo, nicknamed Angel because he had the most angelic demeanor and had looked after his ma in his little-boy way, making her peanut butter and jelly sandwiches, fetching her water, reading his favorite books to her. Vinny swallowed over the lump in his throat. Angel was only in half-day kindergarten, mornings, and today was the first day Vinny wouldn't be there with him after school. His mother-in-law, Loretta, would be home with him, but still. Vinny had even thought about taking his lunch hour at home with them, but he wouldn't have that much time with the commute, and Angel wouldn't understand why he had to leave so soon.

He turned to his assistant, his young cousin Tony. "Leave the mower. We'll stack the boxes against that wall." He gestured where he wanted them, and they got to work.

By noon, he had a pretty good idea what he was dealing with upstairs. He'd need to get the plumber and electrician in here. He and Tony had already reinforced the floor, working around the access panel. After lunch, they'd build the wooden stairs for an outdoor entrance.

"Break for lunch," he told Tony.

They sat in the cab of the truck, windows rolled down on this sunny May day, and ate the sandwiches they'd brought. Vinny filled his cousin in on the next steps for the afternoon's work. When he'd finished lunch, he told Tony, "I'm going to see about using their phone."

"But you said we shouldn't go inside."

Mostly they worked commercial construction, but occasionally to fill in a gap, his dad would take on smaller residential jobs. The rule was to disturb the homeowner as little as possible. "It's for Angel." He'd considered driving to a pay phone, but there weren't pay phones on every corner in a suburb like this. It could take a while to find one, and he didn't want to rush through his call with Angel.

He got out of the truck. Tony lit up a cigarette. Vinny leaned in the window. "Hey. Not in the truck. Go take a walk."

Tony huffed out a breath, but he complied.

Vinny headed for the front door and knocked.

Allison answered, opening the door fully to him, not just a crack like some homeowners did. "Hi! How's it going out there?"

He locked his knees, pushing down the urgent need to get to the phone and make sure his boy was okay. "Everything's great. We reinforced the floor. The structure is sound otherwise. I'll have electrician and plumber in early next week."

"Okay, great." She beamed a smile so bright it broke through his dark haze for a moment. How long had it been since he or anyone around him had smiled like that? Days? Months? Years? Five years of increasingly bad news, a slow build of despair.

"I need to use your phone," he said urgently. "My son just got home from kindergarten, and I need to check in."

"Oh. I'm actually heading out to pick up my son from the kindergarten bus stop. Can you wait twenty minutes for us to get back?"

She didn't want him in her house alone. He understood; they'd just met. Didn't mean he didn't have the urge to shove her out of the way and find the phone on his own. But he knew better. Besides, Angel wasn't expecting his call. It was more to put Vinny's mind at ease. Angel was probably happily eating whatever his Nonna made him for lunch. But would she ask Angel how he was doing? He didn't volunteer everything right up front.

"Twenty minutes," he said, turned and went back to his truck. He'd use the time to line up the lumber they needed. He checked his watch twice, shook it to make sure it was still working, and then finally it was time.

He jogged back to the door and knocked. Thankfully she answered. "It's in the kitchen."

He left his work boots on the front porch and followed her inside, down the hallway to the kitchen on the right, where a little boy with light brown hair and a smudge of dirt on his face stood on a step stool at the sink, where he was probably supposed to be washing his hands, but was instead staring at the strange man in his kitchen, his green eyes too big for his face.

Vinny lifted a hand in greeting.

"Can I try your tools?" the boy asked, staring at Vinny's toolbelt.

Allison spoke up. "Jared, wash your hands. I told you the workers are very busy." She crossed to Vinny and handed him a cordless phone. "You can take it in the dining room for privacy if you'd like." She gestured to an adjoining formal dining room.

He nodded and went into the other room, quickly dialing home. His mother-in-law, Loretta, answered. "Hi, it's Vinny. I just wanted to say hi to Angel, see how his day went."

"I'll get him."

A moment later, his sweet boy's voice came through the line, earnest and pure. "Hi, Daddy! I got a loose tooth!"

He nearly collapsed with relief. He was okay. He sounded happy. "That's great, bud. Did ya have a good day?"

"Uh-huh. I've been wiggling my tooth all day, but it won't come out."

"Don't force it. It'll come out when it's ready."

"Nonna says we can tie a string to my tooth and the door-knob and slam it. Pow! Tooth out."

"No. That's the old way. Now we leave it until it's ready."

"Okay. I hope I get a lot of money from the tooth fairy. Robbie got five dollars!"

"Last time I checked, the tooth fairy left one dollar."

Angel whispered loudly into the phone, "I think the tooth fairy got richer."

"I'd expect one dollar. I think maybe Robbie's parents added some because they got richer. That's not us. How's your lunch?"

"Good. Nonna made my favorite, ziti with cheese dots. When're you coming home?"

His heart clutched. He wanted to drive home that very minute. But he knew he had to prepare Angel for the way things were going to be, back to the normal routine. "I'll see ya at dinner."

"Okay. Bye."

"I love you." The phone made a banging noise. He'd probably run off.

"It's me," Loretta said. "Don't worry, he's doing just fine."

"Okay, thanks again for your help. I'll see ya later." He disconnected and stared at the ceiling, trying to pull it together. Angel was fine. Vince and Nico were still at school, but he knew they'd come home and be fine too. They would all keep going just like they always had. It had been him and Loretta keeping the family going for the past year, taking care of the kids and Maria.

He went into the kitchen. Jared wasn't there, but he could hear the TV in another room. Allison stood at the stove, her back to him, cooking lunch.

"All done," he said.

She whirled. "Oh, hi. Didn't hear you come in over the exhaust fan from the stove. Grilled cheese."

He set the phone on the counter, keeping a polite distance. "Thanks for letting me use your phone."

"No problem. How's your son?"

He rubbed the back of his neck. "He's good. I think I needed the phone call more than he did."

She shook her head, smiling, and he was struck with her sunny brightness—her light blond hair up in a high ponytail, her eyes bright blue, her skin glowing with health. She looked so much younger than him. He was thirty-six, but the past few years had taken a toll, making him feel ancient. "Isn't that just like a kid?" she asked. "They're fine while we're worried sick. Feel free to stop by same time tomorrow if you want to check in with him again."

That small kindness reached in and squeezed his heart. "Thank you. I just might do that."

She nodded once and turned back to the grilled cheese, flipping it over. She was a tiny thing yet radiated so much life. So different from the heavy sense of impending death he'd lived with for so long. He wanted to get closer to that light.

He turned and walked straight out the front door.

2

Vinny returned to Allison's front door the next day at the same time to call Angel. And the day after that. A week later, he couldn't even pretend it was for Angel anymore. He was there for that moment of brief connection in Allison's kitchen, standing there smiling at him, asking after his boy. She understood that close tie of family, that love for your children. His mother-in-law, Loretta, had become irritated with him checking in, but he didn't care. If he wanted to check in, he would.

He felt a little less alone in those brief moments talking to Allison about their kids. She told him about her three boys, close in age to his own, and what they were into. Gabe and Luke loved video games and riding their bikes. Jared, the kindergarten kid, was the daredevil and already skilled at skateboarding. He told her about his boys. Vince and Nico were into sports—football, basketball, and baseball—like him. Angel was just starting in baseball. That one was too shrimpy for football. His wife, Maria, had decreed it, and Vinny honored her request. Vince and Nico were big like him. Those daily talks were the bright spot in his day.

Today was the Friday before the long Memorial Day weekend, and he was looking forward to having the time off to spend with his kids. He went and got the cordless phone himself, Allison already expecting him while she fried up a couple of hot dogs for Jared, acknowledging him with a wave and a smile. He found himself smiling back, a foreign feeling.

He called Angel, asked him about his day, and then Angel unexpectedly touched a nerve. "Gotta go! Nonna and I are working in the garden today."

That had been Maria's garden and hadn't been touched in a year. "What're you doing with it?" he managed over the tightness in his throat.

"First we have to pull weeds; then we're planting new stuff. Bye!" He hung up.

His eyes were suddenly hot. The garden was an eyesore, dead plants, overrun by weeds, but somehow looking at it had reminded him of Maria. Slowly dying as she did. It was morbid but comforting, reflecting back his reality. He took a deep breath and pinched the bridge of his nose, closing his eyes. This was how it should be. The young breathing life into the world. New things should have a chance to grow.

"Can I use your hammer?" a little voice asked.

He opened his eyes to find Jared standing in front of him, pointing at the hammer on Vinny's tool belt. Vinny had a kid-size hammer in his toolbox he let his boys use. "You'll have to ask your mom if it's okay."

"Mom!" he hollered at the top of his lungs. "Can I use the worker's hammer?"

Allison walked in, saying to Jared, "I thought you were watching TV. I told you not to bother the workers. And his name is Mr. Marino." She looked up at Vinny. "Sorry about that."

"It's no problem."

Jared ran back to the living room, probably figuring he had no chance of using a hammer now.

"How's Angel doing today?" she asked.

"Good." His voice caught and he cleared his throat. "He's working in his ma's garden." His throat closed and he needed to get out fast before he broke down. Allison was blocking the way to the kitchen, where he usually put the phone back. He handed her the phone. "Here."

"Is everything okay?"

Nothing would ever be okay again. He met her blue eyes reflecting real concern. In that moment, he needed to share the pain with someone. Sometimes it was too much to keep bottled inside, being strong for his boys.

His voice came out hoarse. "Some days are harder than others. My wife died last month. It's been difficult for all of us."

"Oh, I'm sure it is. I'm so sorry." She stepped closer, her hands lifting, and for a moment he thought she might hug him. But then her hands lowered and she squeezed his hand with her smaller one in a firm warm grip. "Please let me know if there's anything I can do."

"Thank you." There was nothing she could do, but he appreciated the sentiment all the same.

She nodded, releasing his hand, gazing at him with so much sympathy he had to turn from her.

"I'd better get back to work," he muttered and quickly headed out.

He threw himself back into work, trying to keep his focus on anything but what was in his head—young Allison making him feel less alone. He was drawn to her, wanting her comfort, and it pained him that he wanted that from another woman. Maria was his comfort, always had been.

He and Tony were loading up the truck at the end of the day when he felt a soft hand on his arm. He turned to find Allison standing there, holding a covered dish.

"I made you and the boys chicken parmigiana. I thought it would be nice for you to have a break from kitchen duty." She gave him a small smile. "You know, start your long weekend off a little more relaxed."

He never cooked. Loretta left dinner warming in the oven every night, frozen meals in the freezer for the weekend. Allison *cared*. She saw his pain and wanted to lessen the burden.

He took it from her. "Thank you, Allison. I really appreciate it, and I'm sure the boys will too."

"My friends call me Allie."

He cracked a smile, so out of practice it felt strange. "Thank you, Allie."

She leaned close, her hands lifting again for a hug before she backed away. "Sorry. I'm a hugger." She put her hands in the air. "Look out for the strange woman hugging everyone."

"It's nice. Have a good weekend." He lifted the glass container. "Thanks again."

She beamed a smile that made something in him light up too. "Stairs look great!"

He glanced over his shoulder at the stairs they'd built last week. It wasn't the main event. The real work was inside. "Thanks. You should see inside."

She blushed, her gaze falling to his shoulder then his neck then his lips. A sudden awareness of attraction made him stand straighter. He'd only been with one woman, had never even been tempted.

"Have a good weekend," they said at the same time.

She laughed and rushed back to the house. He quickly got into his truck. Tony appeared a moment later from where he'd been tying something down in the back.

He handed over the container for Tony to hold.

Tony lifted it. "What is it?"

"Chicken parm."

"For me?"

"For my kids." *And me. She cared enough to cook for me.*

He dropped Tony off at the construction office, where his car was parked, and drove home, feeling lighter than he had in years. He walked in the door of his ranch home, set the container a safe distance away on the coffee table, and announced, "I'm home!"

The boys rushed in, hugging his legs and middle, all of them talking over each other in their excitement to see him again. He greeted each of them, hugging them close and ruffling their hair.

"What's that?" Loretta asked, appearing from the kitchen in her apron and zeroing in on the food container. Her gray hair was in a bun, her figure stout, and her tone authoritative.

He picked up the container. "The woman at the job I'm working made us some chicken parm for the weekend. I'll just stick it in the freezer." He headed for the kitchen to put it away.

She intercepted before he could get to the freezer, taking the container from him and opening the lid. She frowned. "A woman cooked for you?"

"She said she wanted to give us a break for the weekend."

Loretta sniffed. "What break? I do the cooking around here."

"I know. She was just being nice. I'll freeze it. Maybe we'll have it when you want a day off."

She leaned down and smelled the chicken parm. "It's terrible." She pointed at it. "This isn't even real mozzarella. What is this? American cheese? It's not even real cheese." She yanked the garbage can out from under the sink and dumped it in.

He lurched forward and stopped. Too late. Besides, he understood why. She wanted him to honor his wife's memory, her daughter, not move on to another woman, however innocent their friendship. Guilt sliced at him. He was a grieving widower; he didn't get to have sunshine and light, didn't get the comfort only a woman could give. Not to mention Allie was married. You didn't take comfort from a married woman.

Loretta wiped her hands in an exaggerated gesture of good riddance and set the dish in the sink, pouring water in it to soak. She turned off the faucet and turned to him. "I will teach you how to cook. Real Italian cooking. In this way, the boys will know their mother."

"They've got you," he said. "Nothing's better than Nonna's cooking."

"You will learn," she ordered.

He leaned down and kissed her soft cheek before heading for his shower. She meant well, but he didn't see the point in him cooking. Her real point was, don't let another woman take Maria's place. And she was right. He hadn't even been thinking of Allie that way. Well, maybe for a moment. He'd just been touched deeply that she cared.

He'd honor his wife's memory. Always.

3

———

One year later...

Allie stared out the window of her art studio, sipping her tea, enjoying the early morning light and the quiet. Her three boys were in school full-time. Ever since her art studio had been completed and, in no small part due to Vinny's open admiration of her artwork, she'd fully embraced being an artist. Funny how it took the guy who built the studio of all people to give her the confidence she needed to believe in herself. Once Jared started full-time at school, she'd signed up for an illustration class in the city. She'd decided to become a picture-book illustrator and now had a portfolio of work. In fact, just last month her illustrated work had been published in an Easy Reader series featuring a frog named Finkle. And next weekend she would have her very first art show. Though it was a small venue, it was still an honor for her illustrations of forest animals to be displayed at the Clover Park library.

Unfortunately, the more she'd grown as an artist and a person, the worse her marriage became. Maybe because she had more respect for herself, standing up for what she wanted. She and William used to fight about what he called her neediness—her attempts at conversation and affection—and money. He resented her spending "his" money on nonessentials like the drapes, nice frames for pictures of the kids, and knickknacks to warm up the chilly atmosphere of their home. Now that she'd given up on intimacy, their fights were just about money, more specifically, money she spent on art supplies and her illustration class. He called her illustrations her little cartoon hobby and thought what she'd been paid for the Easy Reader series was pathetic. She'd just been happy to be paid and had stashed the money in a savings account of her own for any future art-related expenses. William wanted her to either get a real job or magically become the corporate wife he needed. He alternated arguing with the intensity of the blood-sucking corporate lawyer he was and keeping a cold distance.

What it came down to was that she was not the wife he wanted anymore. This was made abundantly clear when he took an apartment in the city, saying he was tired of the commute, and only came home on weekends. She suspected he had a mistress. She'd confronted him about it more than once and got nowhere. She was tired of arguing, tired of crying, just so damn tired.

Sometimes she thought of divorce. It wouldn't be all that much different from the way they lived now, but then she'd look at her boys and think she just needed to hang on until the kids were grown. She had to know they would be okay. Jared was only six. She didn't want to rock the foundation of their world. Her own parents were still married, even if they didn't seem all that happy. Divorce had been a dirty word in her household growing up, said only in whispers about other people who'd failed at marriage. Her parents had taught her and her sister that divorce was shameful. It was a hard thing to shake, that feeling of shame and failure.

She set her tea on the table and ran her finger along the beveled edge of the bookcase Vinny had made her to thank her for the dinners she'd given him. She'd cooked Vinny and his boys dinner every Friday while he'd worked here, and he'd always accepted so graciously. It was a little thing, giving him a small break on the weekend, but it was what she could do.

She bent and pulled out the thick art book on color, flipping it to the center, where she'd stashed a holiday card from Marino and Sons Construction. She opened it and ran her finger over the large confident scrawl of Vinny's signature. They'd become friends during the six weeks he'd worked on her art studio, chatting after his call home to his son on Vinny's lunch break. Soon they were chatting when he was done work for the day too. Mostly they talked about their kids, but he was such a good listener she'd confided her dream of becoming an illustrator. She'd even shared some of her early efforts based on classic picture books she admired. The last thing he'd said to her on his last day on the job, with clear respect and admiration in his eyes, was to "keep that fire in your belly, keep going with your art. It's a gift."

She'd cried when he drove off. It had touched her so deeply for someone to really see her and acknowledge her as an artist. Their goodbye had felt bigger somehow than a casual goodbye.

She thought of him often, wondering how he was doing as a single dad to three boys. She hoped his sadness had lessened, that he might have some small joys in his life. Like she did with her art and her boys. He'd only sent this holiday card because she'd sent one to him through his company. She didn't know his home address and hadn't wanted to get too personal. Both Vinny and Tony had signed it. She wasn't sure why she'd kept it, but every once in a while when her thoughts drifted, she pulled it out, remembering his sadness, but also remembering his warmth and encouragement.

That was it. She would invite him to her art show, along with his boys. The illustrations were made for children, after all. She pulled out her sketch pad and drew a quick illustration of a happy-looking golden retriever. Then she added in bold letters: You're Invited to Allie's First Art Show. Next line: Featuring picture-book illustrations of forest creatures. She added the address, date and time she'd be there on Saturday morning, and mentioned she'd be giving out free early readers of the series she'd illustrated.

She mailed it to his work. Either he'd show up or he wouldn't.

She didn't even know if he was local.

He could be busy. Three boys in May were probably crazy busy with baseball games.

She wouldn't get her hopes up.

Vinny drove like a man on a mission. He had exactly thirty minutes to catch Allie's art show. Nico's baseball game had just wrapped up, Angel's was done super early this morning, and he had Vince's game in the afternoon. His boys were in their baseball uniforms in the backseat of the minivan, quiet with their mouths full of deli subs. He'd been so happy for Allie when he got her invitation in the mail. She'd wanted to be an illustrator and she'd made it. Her own art show, her own published books that she'd illustrated. He knew she had talent and was thrilled to see how far she'd come in only a year.

He'd never forgotten her kindness, asking after his boys, cooking for them every week to give him a break. It hadn't given him a break since Loretta wouldn't stand for it, but he'd accepted the offer gratefully every week and given it to his bachelor cousin Tony, who was equally grateful to have a home-cooked meal. The irony was, now Vinny really was the cook in the family. His father-in-law's health had taken a turn for the worse, and Loretta had become a full-time nurse for her husband. She'd given Vinny a crash course in Italian cooking and then followed up, having him and the boys go to her place for supervised cooking every Sunday. He now made a pretty mean sauce and had become a whiz at ravioli. That was what his boys liked best, so he made it often, secretly hiding vegetables in the cheese filling.

The note he'd written Allie burned a hole in his jeans pocket. He wasn't sure what had come over him, putting his deepest thoughts into words, but he didn't know when he'd ever have a chance to see her again, and he just wanted her to know how much she'd helped him during a dark time of his life. Still helped him when the darkness closed in.

A crumpled paper wrapper shot into the cup holder next to him from one of the boys. He glanced back at the big hand of his oldest, ten-year-old Vince. "Don't put your trash up front. Stick it in the bag it came in."

Vince complied, making a big noise about it. "How quiet do we gotta be to get ice cream after my game?"

"Library quiet," Vinny said. "Whisper."

"I'm a great whisperer!" six-year-old Angel shouted, his Ss lisping with his missing front teeth.

"That's not a whisper," Nico said, then lowered his voice. "This is a whisper. We're gonna look at pictures an artist made and have ice cream."

"Her name is Allie Reynolds," he told them. Just saying her name sent a zing of anticipation through him. She'd remembered him after all this time, and that meant something. Maybe she'd enjoyed their talks as much as he had. Or maybe that had just been a matter of circumstance. He'd been depressed and she'd been a bright light of caring and comfort. He wasn't depressed anymore, but he wasn't exactly happy either.

Angel whispered so softly he couldn't make out what he was saying.

Vince piped up. "Yeah, who is Allie? Is she famous?"

He cleared his throat. "She's an artist friend. I built her an art studio last year."

"Is she rich?" Nico asked.

"No, not rich, but not poor either." She was married to a lawyer. Her husband had signed the check for the construction work—William Reynolds, Esquire. "Maybe one day she'll be famous for her artwork."

"Cool!" Nico exclaimed. "I'm gonna have her sign my free book."

Vinny smiled. "That would be great. We're just hitting the tail end of her show though. They might be out of the free books."

"Hit the gas!" Nico exclaimed.

"Yeah, make her fly!" Vince hollered.

He sped up a little, almost as eager as his kids for reasons he didn't want to think too much about.

They made it with twenty minutes to spare. The boys ran ahead of him to the library entrance. It was an old brick building with a generic boxy addition tacked on the back sometime in the sixties. He stepped inside the front entrance, the old historic part of the library, scanning the foyer, and spotted Allie to the right in a cozy room with a fireplace and several chairs for reading. Probably the fireplace had been needed back in the day for heat. Her blond head was bent over a book she was signing for a mom and her little girl. Her hair was down, straight past her shoulders, and she wore a light purple tank top with black straps that showed lots of creamy skin. She looked relaxed, smiling at the girl. She didn't look like a mom at all. She looked like an artist.

She looked like a beautiful woman.

For a moment he just stood there, completely enthralled.

A shuffle to his left alerted him to Vince and Nico shoving each other. At ten and eight years old, they could really get into it, especially when they got bored. He grabbed a hold of Vince by the sleeve, separating them, and jerked his head for the other two to follow him into the room. Allie hadn't noticed them yet, still talking to the young girl at her table, so he took a few minutes to look around. Instead of bookcases, the room was lined on opposite sides with magazine racks. Her artwork hung in frames above the magazines and on either side of the fireplace. Beautifully realistic forest scenes that drew you in.

"Here it is," he whispered to the boys. "All of this is her work."

"Where's the free books?" Nico whispered.

He pointed to where Allie was now sitting at the table alone. She looked up, her face lighting up with a smile that made his heart kick up a notch. She jumped up and closed the distance between them. She wore a black skirt, her bare legs in chunky black sandals, her petite body shown to perfection in the snug-fitting clothes. A jolt of lust gripped him so unexpectedly he couldn't breathe for a moment. Like he'd just been jolted back to life.

"You came!" she exclaimed, stopping in front of him. She lifted her hands to hug him, and he shifted a fraction closer, hoping she would. She gave him a quick squeeze and pulled away, smiling down at Angel. "You must be Angel. Your daddy called you every day when he was working on my art studio."

"Hi," Angel whispered.

Vinny smiled. "I told the boys to whisper in the library." He gestured to his other two standing to the side, looking all around. "This is Vince." Vince turned at his name. "And Nico."

Allie smiled at them. "Very nice to meet you. I set aside three books just in case you stopped by."

"You did all these yourself?" Vince asked, pointing at the framed artwork. "Or were the drawings already there and you painted them?"

Allie looked around, beaming and beautiful, even more full of life than when he'd met her a year ago. "I did the drawings and I painted them too."

"Cool," Vince said.

"Come on, I'll get your books." She walked back to her table, a bounce in her step. He watched her go for a moment, realized he was setting a bad example the way he was checking her out, and followed, his eyes glued to the back of her head. Her hair was golden in the sun streaming through the front window, streaks of various shades of blond.

Angel grabbed his hand, holding it tight as they walked. "I gotta pee."

Vinny sighed. Every frigging time. He'd told him to pee at the deli, but he'd said he didn't have to. "Can ya hold it?"

"It's an emergency," Angel whispered.

Vince and Nico were ahead of them, already at the table with Allie. They turned around, each of them staring at the books, looking embarrassed. Vince crossed to him and whispered, "Dad, these are baby books."

"I don't want mine," Nico said, giving it to Angel.

"That's rude," Vinny hissed. "Gimme. I'll hold them." The boys handed them over. "Angel, I'll get you your own book. Vince, take your brother to the bathroom."

"It's Nico's turn," Vince whined.

"You're the oldest; that means you help the youngest." Vinny put Angel's hand in Vince's. "Go!"

"Man!" Vince said. "All the work being the oldest, none of the fun."

Angel bounced from foot to foot.

"Come on, little man," Vince said and bent a little so Angel could climb on his back. He ran off, Angel laughing with delight at the unexpected fast ride.

Nico grabbed a car magazine and took a seat, flipping through it, looking very adult for an eight-year-old.

Vinny blew out a breath and walked over to Allie, who was smiling at him again.

He found himself smiling back. "Always an emergency bathroom run to add to the fun."

She laughed. "Believe me, I've been there. The worst is when you're in line at the supermarket, all your food on the conveyor belt, and then suddenly they have to go. Of course, the bathroom is in the basement in the farthest corner from the register. The things we do for our kids!"

He leaned close to confide, "Once I made the mistake of telling Vince to go outside when he was four and then spent the next year trying to stop him from going outside whenever he felt like it."

Her blue eyes lit up, and he knew in that instant why he was so drawn to her. So much life and good humor. It made him feel good just looking at her. "You do it once," she said, "then it's fair game."

He smiled, shaking his head. "I'm really impressed with your work. It's beautiful." *And so are you.*

She flushed and smoothed her hair, looking away and then back. "Thank you."

"Could I get a book signed to Angel?"

"Of course!" She pulled one out and signed it, handing it over. "I don't know if I ever told you how much it meant to me to have you encourage me to keep going with my art. I'm in a much better place now because of your kind words."

"Aww, I'm sure that was all you. You're the one with the talent. Anyone can see that."

She gazed at him with real affection. "Thank you again. I really did appreciate it and your coming here today too. Your boys are sweet."

He laughed. "I don't know that I'd call them sweet. But they're good kids. Your boys didn't come today?"

"Their dad dropped them off earlier. They lasted all of five minutes. It's not a big deal for them. They've seen all my stuff tons of times and already have the books."

Their dad dropped them off. Did that mean a divorce situation? Allie had confided once that her relationship with her husband was rocky. "Did your husband stick around a bit?"

Her expression closed. "No, he's not very supportive of work that brings so little money. He waited outside."

"It's not about the money," he snapped, irritated on her behalf. "It's about using your gift, doing what you were meant to do."

She blinked rapidly and blew out a breath. "How've you been, Vinny? Really. You hanging in there okay?"

He shoved his hands in his pockets, his fingers colliding with the note. He left it there. "I'm okay. My mother-in-law has been busy taking care of my father-in-law, so I learned to cook. He's not doing so well."

"I'm sorry to hear it."

"Yeah. I had to get a babysitter for the boys." He nodded once. "We're all hanging in there."

She gave him a small sympathetic smile. "I'm impressed you're a cook now on top of being a great dad and master carpenter."

He flushed at the compliment. She knew how much the boys meant to him, and she'd raved over the bookcase he'd made her as a spur-of-the-moment parting gift. He took his hands out of his pockets, gesturing while he talked. "Just simple stuff. Homemade sauce, ravioli, ziti, manicotti."

"All the best Italian cooking. I wish I could cook like that."

He almost offered to teach her, but then he realized no. She was married. The wedding vows were sacred to him. He had no right to start something with her; he had to think of his kids first and foremost, be the parent they needed him to be.

"Vinny, would you like to get a cup of coffee sometime?" she asked softly. "Just, you know, catch up and talk."

He looked into her blue eyes and saw longing. She wanted to get closer to him just like he was drawn in, wanting more of her. No good could come of this. There was something there, something way beyond the bounds of friendship, and he had to back off. Spending time together would only encourage that spark to ignite.

He swallowed hard. "I don't think that would be a good idea."

"Oh." She leaned back, her expression pinched. "Okay."

Shit. The last thing he wanted to do was hurt her feelings. "I only say that because..." He stuck his hand in his pocket, palmed the note, and grabbed her hand, shaking it and giving it to her at the same time. "I'm not interested in you as a friend. Goodbye."

Her eyes widened, her hand closing around the note. "Goodbye," she whispered.

He turned and walked away, his legs a little wobbly over the risk he just took. He snagged Nico on his way out just as Vince appeared in the foyer, holding Angel by the hand.

"Let's go," Vinny said.

"Do we get ice cream?" Vince asked.

"Yup. You guys did great."

"Yeah!" "Woo!" "Ice cream!" they hollered, still inside the library.

He was too preoccupied with his thoughts to bother telling them to quiet down. Because he'd just told Allie that when he couldn't sleep at night, when the darkness closed in, he thought of her and her light, and it brought him peace.

He'd bared his soul knowing he could never see her again.

4

Allie kept her note from Vinny inside her art book with his holiday card, a secret treasure hidden in a safe place. This big burly construction worker man had soul. His dark brown eyes framed with thick lashes that once radiated sadness should've given her a clue. Now his eyes showed such warmth. And his smile—flashing white against his olive skin with a hint of stubble along his strong jaw—was a welcome unexpectedly sexy sight. His low roll of laughter had sprung joy in her heart.

She'd never met a man who could express himself so openly. And to know that she had an effect on him, that she'd brought him peace when he'd needed it most, it was nothing short of a miracle. Somehow despite all the barriers between them, all the surface differences in their lives and circumstances, they'd connected. And, a year later, were still connected. How could that be after not seeing each other for so long?

She had to write back.

She waited until Monday morning with her husband gone for the week back in the city, her boys at school, in the quiet of her art studio. She got out paper and pen and stopped. She didn't have his home address. She couldn't mail a note to his work the way she had with her art invitation. Anyone might open it, and this was more personal. She shook her head at herself. What was she thinking that they would be pen pals?

He'd bared his soul, telling her how much she'd meant to him. They'd only known each other six weeks. Imagine if they'd had more time together.

She could look him up. She didn't know which town he lived in, though, and wasn't sure how many Marinos were in the area.

You know what? She was going to write back. Didn't mean she had to send it.

Dear Vinny,

The first time we met, I was stunned by the sadness in your eyes. Because I've felt a bone-deep sadness like that too. And I know now what you've been through and know that my pain can't even come close to yours. I'm so sorry for your loss.

But I do know what it's like to feel sad, lonely, trapped in my marriage. I dropped out of college, pregnant, and married in a hurry. You know what they say, marry in haste, repent in leisure. Well, it's true.

You too were a light in the darkness for me. I was losing myself, and then focusing on you and your pain as you built something so important to me, my art studio, somehow it made it all come together, and you became the light for me. You made me believe in myself, in my talent, and I'll be forever grateful for that. I'm thirty-two years old and I'm finally figuring out what I'm meant to do with my life.

I understand why you hesitate to meet with me, a married woman, because I've felt it too. That energy between us that is…more. I wish we had met under different circumstances.

Keep on being the wonderful father and man you are.

Allie

She tucked the letter inside her art book, next to his, imagining they were having the conversation they would never have in real life.

Madness.

Back to work. No more letters, no more daydreaming, no more what-ifs.

But something had changed for her with that simple note from Vinny. She spent the week in a fog, for the first time questioning what would make her happy. Would she be happier free of her marriage? Maybe. But she had to be doing it for the right reasons. Not for Vinny, which might not even work out. It wasn't just her she had to think about, it was her children. She was sure she'd have full custody, William had little interest in his sons, but she'd have to fight for alimony. Things would be tight. Illustration work wouldn't begin to cover the bills. She'd need a full-time job, giving up her time with the kids, giving up her time for her art. She'd be trading a certain life for uncertainty, and she feared the fallout for her boys.

By Friday morning, after she'd seen the boys off to school, she was clear on what she should do, which was absolutely nothing. The status quo was what her kids needed, and she'd find her happiness in her art. That was the sensible thing to do. The right thing.

She opened the door to her art studio and slapped a hand over her mouth.

An envelope with her name on it was on the floor in front of her. She recognized Vinny's big confident scrawl. He'd slipped it under the door either late last night or early this morning. Last night was a school night. It must've been this morning, maybe on his way to work.

With trembling fingers, she picked it up and locked the door behind her. Her heart pounded in her ears as she slipped the letter from the envelope. It was short and to the point.

Allie,
    I should've said this when I saw you. If things change for you, get in touch for that cup of coffee.
    Vinny

He left his phone number and address.

She stood there for a solid minute, staring at the scrawled

note, before leaping into action. She tucked his note in her art book, took the letter she'd written but never sent, and promptly addressed it, added a stamp, and walked down the street, dropping it into the mailbox.

The moment she shut the mailbox flap, regret seized her. She pulled it open again and tried to take it back, her arm jammed in the narrow space, grasping at air. She peered inside. Everything was so dark she couldn't even see it in there.

Shit. What did she just start?

Dear Allie,

I was happy to get your letter. I guess we were what each other needed at the right time. I figure if I was still working over there, I'd ask you about your boys, so how're they doing? Gabe and Luke still crazy about Mario? How's Jared doing with his skateboarding? I hope he hasn't gotten stuck in any more trees. My boys are good. Vince is showing a great arm as a pitcher, and Nico just hit a grand slam in last night's game. Angel's doing well too, though the coach had to tell him to face the ball more than once. He keeps looking down at third base, playing in the dirt. Maybe baseball isn't his sport.

How're you? Are you working on a new book series? I hope to see your work in a lot of books. I'm sure it'll make a lot of kids happy to see it. It's beautiful, realistic but better than reality, if that makes sense. I'm rambling.

I'm hanging in there, busy like always with work and the boys. Can't complain. Everyone's healthy. Except my father-in-law. He's been sent to a hospice. Life's short. Now I'm depressing myself, so I'll sign off. Paint some sunshine for me. I could use a little of your light in my life.

Vinny

Vinny,

Enclosed is your requested sunshine. I used colored pencil

for this one. Sorry about your father-in-law. Life sucks sometimes.

My boys are doing well. All three just got report cards with straight As. I'm sensing some college bills in my future. Maybe if I sell a kidney. Ha! Or a million books. I'm sending my portfolio to a bunch of publishers, hoping for contract work. Maybe one day I'll create the text to go with my illustrations and then I'd get the whole royalty instead of half. Just have to think of some cute concept kids would like. Somehow I don't think eat your vegetables and go to bed on time will catch on.

I think of you often and hope life is treating you well.

Gabe came home with a black eye from a bully at school. The other boy was suspended. I'm not sure what to do to keep it from happening again. His dad says he needs to toughen up. I think maybe I should put him in a different school. What would you do?

Allie

Allie,

Here's what I would do. Talk to the bully's parents about it not happening again. Then I would talk to Gabe about self-defense. He has to know the basics, blocking a punch, throwing a punch with his thumb tucked on the outside of his fingers, not in. Sometimes the only thing that stops a bully is giving him a taste of his own medicine. If his dad can't teach him the basics, take Gabe to someone who can. Maybe go to a karate class if it comes down to it. And tell him to make friends with the biggest boy in his class. How you think I got so popular?

Tell me about you, how you spend your days, when you're at your happiest. I like picturing it.

Vinny

Vinny,

Well, no more black eyes. Gabe says everything's okay now. I hope that's true. I took him to a karate class, but he hated it so much he didn't make it past the two-week free-trial period. He made friends with the biggest kid in his class, Shane, who is a very nice boy with the brightest red hair.

I'm at my happiest painting in the early morning light with music blasting in the background, something with a good beat I can rock out to.

When are you at your happiest?

Allie

Allie,

I'm at my happiest when I get a letter from you.

Vinny

She pressed the letter to her heart, her eyes welling. It had had that effect on her the first time she'd read it, and now rereading it for the millionth time after a year of letters, it was just as powerful. Simple, to the point, yet it grabbed her by the throat.

A *year* of letters.

Too many to tuck in a book. She kept them tied with a pink ribbon, hidden in the storage space above her studio. Her letters had been mailed down the street, his hand-delivered early Friday morning. Innocent letters yet not. She yearned for more. She wanted to see him, hear him, be with him. The distance between them was a problem that only she could fix. She wrote him one final letter, knowing he'd read between the lines.

Vinny,

I have a very difficult decision to make due to our deepening friendship. I will be in touch to let you know how things turn out. This will be my last letter until then. Please do not write back. I need to think.

Allie

Vinny respected her wishes. She didn't hear from him. She waited another month to be sure she was doing it for the right reasons, and then finally she faced William. He returned home late Friday night from the city. She'd arranged for the boys to spend the night at her parents' house.

For the first time in a long while, she studied her husband as he walked into the kitchen, always his first stop home. He looked much older than his thirty-nine years. He ran his own law firm now with a partner, just as he'd wanted from the moment he'd graduated with his law degree. He worked an insane number of hours, and it was taking its toll. His light brown hair was thinning, he had bags under his eyes, lines in his face, and his skin was pale and sallow, like he hadn't seen the sun in years. He mostly napped when he was home on the weekend or watched TV. For a moment she almost felt bad for throwing a wrench in his life. He probably wanted nothing more than to eat a late dinner and sit in front of the TV. But now she had to think of her needs not his. She'd found an affordable local lawyer to help her, though she knew William with his legal expertise would not make this easy.

She took a deep breath as he brushed past her on his way to the refrigerator. "William, I want a divorce."

He turned to face her; his expression unchanged, tired and weary. Maybe they'd both known it was inevitable. "Okay."

"Okay." She let out a shaky breath. "I'd like full custody of the kids."

"Done. I'll say goodbye to them this weekend and move permanently to the city."

Her gut clenched at his complete indifference. "You don't sound surprised. Or upset about it. This was a difficult decision for me."

He ran a hand through his hair. "I think we both know this marriage died long ago."

"Why didn't you say anything?"

He lifted one shoulder. "You're a good mother. I thought that would be enough."

Agitation rose in her. "Would you have divorced me if I didn't say anything?"

His lips pressed into a flat line. "I thought it would be better if it was mutual."

Probably for legal reasons. Her temper flared. "Well, it definitely is!"

He looked around the kitchen, let out a sigh, and said, "I guess I'll be going out to eat tonight. When will the kids be home?"

"Tomorrow by noon."

"I'll stop by then to say goodbye. My lawyer will be in touch with you on Monday morning. Goodbye, Allie."

"Goodbye."

He left, just as cold and distant as ever.

She stared at the floor. Not one shred of shame or sense of failure went through her. His cold dismissal had only confirmed she'd done the right thing. A sob bubbled up. She sank to the floor and cried for all the wasted time, for all the misery she'd waded through, thinking she was doing what was best for her kids, when none of it mattered. He was a cold hard man with no love for her at all. She wasn't even sure if he loved their children. The only time he warmed to the kids was when they brought home good report cards. He wanted them to follow in his footsteps and join his law firm. But did he ever think about what was best for them? What they wanted to do with their lives?

After a while, she calmed and returned to her art studio, where she always felt happiest. Maybe she'd have to move when this was all said and done, but she had her little art studio now.

She'd know her future better on Monday morning.

5

———

A month passed.

Then another month.

Three months.

When it got to be four months, Vinny had to face facts. Allie had made her decision. She didn't want to shake up her life, and he understood why. First and always was the kids' welfare. So no more letters. He needed to move on. Not that he wanted to date. This thing with Allie had been so much more than that, a deeply meaningful friendship like she'd said.

Fridays always reminded him of her. That was the day she'd give him a home-cooked meal and also the day he'd stopped by her art studio to slip a letter under the door. Now it was nothing.

He drove home from work, thinking ahead to the weekend. It was September and the boys were back to school and sports. Vince and Nico had football games. Angel had soccer. Life was good. He had things to look forward to; his life was very full with the kids.

He pulled into the driveway, parked, and got the mail. He rifled through the usual bills and junk and then froze. A letter from Allie. His adrenaline kicked in—heart pounding, sweat beading on his forehead. He got back in the truck and stared at it for a moment before ripping it open.

> Vinny,
>
> My divorce is now official. This wasn't because of you. I've been very unhappy for years. My boys have been acting out during their visits to their dad every other weekend, but are otherwise fine at home. I have full custody, as I hoped, and got the house, which I wanted to keep the boys' lives as unchanged as possible.
>
> All this to say, I'm in a much better place now. How about that cup of coffee?
>
> Allie

Joy spiked through him, quickly followed by nerves. This was an invitation to start something. He'd been devoted to one woman since he was seventeen years old. He was thirty-eight now. Would Maria be okay with him seeing another woman? Would his mother-in-law, who was still very involved in his and the boys' life, be okay with it? Could his boys, who still missed their ma, handle him moving on? Was *he* ready to move on?

He swallowed hard. Now he had a difficult decision to make.

That night Vinny did something he hadn't done in a long time. He pulled out the framed picture of his wedding day from his nightstand drawer and set it on the nightstand. It had hurt him to look at it before, seeing the two of them so young and happy, thinking their whole lives were ahead of them together. Maria had been gone more than two years now, but it felt like longer. She'd been fading away for five years before that, only a wisp of her former vibrant self.

The boys were asleep, but he still didn't speak out loud. Instead he looked at her picture and spoke to her in his head. He confessed how lonely he'd been, how sad, how he couldn't sleep sometimes with the burden of grief and responsibility he carried. He asked her permission to move on.

He got nothing from it.

She was just gone, and no amount of wishing or hoping or praying was going to change that.

He spent the rest of the weekend agitated. He didn't like not having a definite decision on what to do. He liked a clear way forward, but as he spent his time cheering for his kids from the sidelines, doing the Sunday errands of food shopping and new clothes for Vince, he knew only one thing—he wanted to see Allie again. He didn't know if that meant for a cup of coffee or a relationship or what. He waffled back and forth on his intentions. He wanted to be clear because the last thing he wanted was to hurt her.

Sunday dinner at his in-laws' house had him in charge of cooking as usual. For the first time, Loretta didn't supervise him at all. Instead she sat in the living room, holding her husband's hand as he rested in a recliner. His father-in-law, Mike, had been sent home from the hospice to die in the comfort of his own home. His boys sat on the sofa, all of them watching a game show.

After he set the food on the dining room table—two pans of lasagna, warm Italian garlic bread, and salad—Loretta declared he was now an official Italian chef. Only took two years and change plus many scoldings, but he'd graduated.

"Thanks, Loretta. It was all your great recipes." She wrote nothing down, all of it top secret, only shared one person to another.

"You did good, Vinny," she said. "You did what you should for your boys so they know their mother's cooking."

"This is Ma's recipe?" Vince asked.

"They're family recipes," Loretta replied. "Passed down the generations. And now I taught your dad to keep the tradition going. Hopefully he'll teach you boys one day or your wives."

Vince curled his lip in disgust. "Wives! Blech."

"Gross," Nico put in.

"I wanna get a wife," Angel declared, which made them all laugh. He had a long way to go from first grade to wife.

Loretta shook her finger at the boys. "Vince and Nico, you might feel very differently in a few years."

"No way!" Vince proclaimed. Nico heartily agreed.

He and Loretta exchanged an amused look. Mike remained in his recliner, watching TV. He ate very little now.

After dinner, Loretta went to wash dishes, as she usually did. That was the deal. Vinny cooked; Loretta cleaned up. But this time Vinny followed her in, offering to dry while she washed.

They worked together in silence for several minutes before she turned to him. "What is it?"

"What do you mean?"

"You're here for a reason. What is it?"

"You doing okay? I mean, with Mike and everything."

She took a deep breath and looked to the ceiling and then back to him. "It will be a blessing for him. He's in pain and tired of suffering. For me? I will grieve. I will honor his memory. And I will carry on for my grandchildren as long as I can." She was a strong woman.

"I'm sorry."

She gave his arm a squeeze. "You and I have been through the wringer. First Maria, now Mike. I didn't think I'd live through Maria's passing."

"I had to for the boys."

She gave him a small smile. "Me too."

She went back to washing dishes, and his mind wandered back to Allie. He'd lost so much, life was so damn short, and he wanted her light in his life.

He spoke over the lump in his throat. "I met someone."

Loretta stilled and turned off the water. She didn't look at him, just stared straight ahead. "Who?"

"Her name is Allie. She's a single mom with three sons close in age to mine."

She closed her eyes as if pained.

"Loretta?"

"Is it serious?"

"We haven't gone on a date yet. I've been thinking about it. I'm not sure if it's the right thing for the boys. I know they miss their ma. I miss her too." His shoulders drooped. "I don't know." Sadness weighed him down again.

She yanked the faucet up, blasting the water, and began furiously scrubbing a pan. Clearly she didn't want him moving on from her daughter, but he'd been so lonely. Maria had been everything, and then there was nothing.

"Loretta."

She ignored him.

He rubbed the back of his neck. "I'd be careful. I wouldn't even introduce the kids until I knew for sure it was a definite thing. I wouldn't let them be hurt by another loss."

She turned, her eyes narrowed. "Do not *speak* to me of another woman."

She returned to the dishes, her movements jerky. Some part of him had been hoping for her blessing, almost like he had Maria's blessing. He let out a breath, turned, and left the kitchen, not at all sure of the right thing to do.

Allie waited nervously in the entryway of a diner in Eastman just after noon on Monday. Vinny got her letter on Friday, and now here she was only three days later about to meet a man with the potential for more for the first time in years. She'd married so young, only nineteen, and had Gabe at twenty. She'd only ever slept with one man. Her heart raced. Maybe she wasn't ready for this.

She ran a shaking hand through her hair. Vinny was working on an office building across the street and would be here at any moment. He'd called her last night. It was the first time they'd spoken by phone, and her belly had actually fluttered from his warm deep voice in her ear. She'd hung up and spent half the night worked up about seeing him today. She hadn't seen him in person in more than a year. All those letters, her only connection to him.

"Allie?"

She whirled, heat rushing to her cheeks. He was here, the

soulful letter writer, the bulky-with-muscles man. She took a moment to soak him in. His dark hair, dark eyes, and tanned olive skin were a striking contrast to his white T-shirt. His shoulders were massive, his chest broad, his legs long in faded jeans with work boots. All of him was so big everywhere, much bigger than her. His physicality struck her in a whole different light now, what that might feel like close up. She broke out in goose bumps, a primal response to unknown territory.

He flashed a smile that lit up his gorgeous face, his dark brown eyes warm on hers. And then she remembered his devotion to his sons, to his wife's memory, and she knew this was just as big a step for him as her.

She moved forward without hesitation and wrapped her arms around his middle in a warm hug. He hugged her back and then pulled away, giving her a small smile. "Ready for coffee?"

The question suddenly felt like it meant so much more. Her heart pounded in her ears. Was she ready for this?

"Yes."

Their gazes locked for an intense moment.

She couldn't hold the eye contact and looked away, her breathing a little fast. She had to calm down. It was just coffee. No promises of more. He signaled the hostess they were ready to be seated.

Allie needn't have worried about coffee with Vinny, which soon turned into lunch. They picked up right where they'd left off, catching each other up on their lives, mostly talking about their kids, but also what she'd been working on. She'd completed three picture books as illustrator since they'd last spoken. He shared about his father-in-law's decline, which she was sad to hear about, and that he'd married his high school sweetheart, which surprised her. Was he just as inexperienced at this dating thing as she was?

"I've only been with one man," she blurted, her cheeks flaming. *Shut up!* God, she was worse than a teenager on her first date. She'd slipped into awkwardly horny mom-on-a-date territory. So embarrassing.

He leaned close and lowered his voice. "I've only been with one woman. I guess we have that in common."

She nodded, calming down a little, relieved she wasn't alone in the anxiety and excitement of dipping her toe in the dating pool. "You seem so relaxed I never would've guessed you were new at this too."

He inclined his head. "I just feel lucky to have met you. I've never even been tempted by another woman in all these years."

Her belly fluttered, her heart pounding. She licked her lips and he watched the movement. Her insides clenched in response, her mind drawing a complete blank. "I-I don't know what to say. I'm a little bit overwhelmed."

He smiled, a charming sexy smile that made the butterflies in her belly go wild. "Say you'll have dinner with me on Saturday night."

She hadn't seen him smile much before. He was devastatingly handsome. She would've found that intimidating if she hadn't connected with him under different circumstances. But she knew this man, knew him on a deeper level than most people in her life. "I would love to. I need to find a babysitter, but I'll let you know."

He flashed a wide smile. "Great."

"Vinny, you are breathtaking."

He laughed, his dark eyes twinkling with good humor. "I've never been called that before. Thanks."

"I'd love to paint you with that smile on your face."

"Keep putting that smile on my face and you can."

She blushed, staring at the table, running her finger along the edge. "I'm so out of practice, dating at thirty-three. My first date since I was a teenager."

"Same here, except I'm thirty-eight. We'll figure it out together."

She met his eyes. He understood. "We'll have to work around the kids. I don't think they're ready to see their mom dating. Their dad moved out four months ago, but still. It's a lot."

"So we'll work around the kids."

"Did you ever think the first time we met that one day we'd be planning our first date?"

"No."

She stared at the table, shaking her head. "Me either."

He lifted her hand to his lips and grazed a kiss across her knuckles, bringing a tingle of electric warmth up her arm. His dark eyes locked on hers. "But I'm glad we are."

6

———

This was only his second first date, and Vinny had the gift of money this time around, so he made reservations at a nice seafood restaurant, figuring Allie was probably used to eating at nice places. He wouldn't even flinch if she ordered lobster. It occurred to him that she was probably used to having gobs of money from her lawyer ex, and while he was doing okay, he wasn't exactly rolling in it. Once his dad retired next June, he'd be in a better position. His dad would name him partner, and Vinny would take over the business. His older brother would've gotten half, but he'd moved to Texas to work on petroleum machinery and never looked back.

He was lucky Loretta had agreed to babysit tonight, though he hadn't told her it was for a date exactly, he just said he was going to dinner. She knew what he was up to, dressing nice for dinner, a bundle of nerves, but she'd drawn the line—no talk of another woman—and he'd respected that. He couldn't ask for more from his mother-in-law. So what if she gave him a curfew, saying he had to pick up the kids by nine since she needed her sleep. He couldn't take that personally; she was an old woman with a sick husband. No way he was turning down free babysitting. If things with Allie progressed, well, he'd deal with the mother-in-law complication later. He clenched his jaw. Things could get very, very difficult with Loretta. The woman was a force and deeply involved in his family's life. He blew out a breath. He couldn't worry about that right now, he had enough to worry about just trying to pull off this date without making a fool of himself.

He drove to Allie's house in his minivan, the same house where they'd first met in what had been a much darker time for both of them. They deserved a little happiness, didn't they? Nerves shot through him. He glanced around the minivan he'd recently cleaned. He'd debated taking his work truck, ultimately deciding neither one was a sexy option. The truck was too dirty for a classy woman like her. Besides, she had kids, she knew the drill. He turned the radio to the game, distracting himself from his nerves, managing to keep his cool.

He parked in the driveway of her house, a large Victorian set on a huge lot with a six-foot privacy fence around the backyard. Great yard for the kids, he figured, maybe a dog too if anyone had time to take care of one.

He got to the front door, rang the bell and, in those few minutes of waiting, completely lost his cool, breaking out in a sweat. He was really on a date. First time since he was a damn teenager and he near felt like one.

She opened the door, standing there in a gray sleeveless dress cut low in front, ending mid-thigh. So sexy. She was tiny, but she had gentle curves in all the right places. Her blond hair was smooth and straight just past her shoulders. A colorful butterfly necklace caught his eye near her throat. Her pulse beat rapidly, visible under the fair skin of her neck. Maybe she was as nervous as he was. Silly when you thought about it. They'd been friends for two years now, though not much of that time had been spent in person.

He lifted his eyes to her bright blues. She smiled, a small shy smile, looking up at him under her lashes. "Hi," she said softly.

"I changed my shirt three times," he blurted.

She laughed. "I like what you decided on. Black's a nice look on you." He wore a black button-down shirt with black pants and his nice dress shoes.

"I love your dress."

Her cheeks flushed. "I bought it special. The necklace too. Symbolic for spreading my wings and living my life the way I want to."

Spreading my wings and other things. A vision of spreading her legs sent a surge of lust through him that he ruthlessly pushed down. Not cool to start a first date with a noticeable woody.

He looked away, rubbing the back of his neck. "That's good. Ready?"

She stepped out, locking the door behind her. "I almost didn't have a babysitter tonight. My usual girl had a last-minute job interview at the mall. Then I was asking my friends for their babysitters, and no one was available. I had to drive an hour out to my parents' house and drop the kids off with them."

He took her hand, walking her to his car. "You must've really wanted to go on this date."

She smiled. "I guess so."

"Me too." He opened the passenger-side door for her, getting an eyeful of slim leg before closing it behind her.

So far, so good. He got in, started the car, and backed out of her driveway. "I made reservations at a seafood restaurant. You like seafood, I hope?"

"Yes."

Silence fell.

He couldn't think of a damn thing to say. He debated putting the game back on, but thought she probably wouldn't be interested. He didn't want to talk about the kids. He wanted this to be about them.

"How was your day?" she asked.

"Good. Usual Saturday runaround with the boys."

"You know what? Let's not do the small-talk thing. I want to get to know you better than that."

"Fine by me, and let's not talk about the kids. Ask me anything."

"Where did you grow up? What was your family like? Did you always want to work construction? What sport is your favorite? What would you do if you had all the time and money in the world?"

He blew out a breath. "That's a lot of questions."

"Just off the top of my head. You don't have to answer if you don't feel comfortable."

"I'm an open book. Let's see, I grew up in the town I live in now, South Norfolk. It's not as nice now as it was when I was a kid, more crime, the schools are going downhill, but I can afford a house there, and my mother-in-law lives in town, so that's a big help. Yes, construction was always for me, it's been in my family for three generations now, and I was taught from the time I could hold a hammer how to use tools. I like working with my hands, I like building something lasting."

"Like building my art studio."

He inclined his head. "That was good for you, but not real challenging. The office building we're doing now is cool, building from the ground up. Now that's a challenge, and it'll stand the test of time. What else? Oh, my family. Just my dad locally now. We get along well. My older brother lives in Texas. My ma, she passed away when I was fifteen."

"Oh, Vinny, I'm so sorry."

"Yeah. It was sudden, one of those freak things. Brain aneurysm. She didn't suffer."

"Gosh, I didn't mean to bring up a painful subject."

"It's okay. It's part of me, and you wanted to get to know me. Keep going with the questions."

"You sure?"

He gestured her on. "Yeah, yeah."

"Favorite sport?"

He grinned. "Football. I was varsity as a freshman. I fucking loved it." He checked in with her right quick. "I mean frigging."

"You don't have to censor yourself with me."

"Allie, you're a classy lady. I don't think I've ever heard you swear."

"Fucking, fucking, fucking."

He got hot hearing that come out of her sweet mouth. He stopped at a stop sign and looked at her. She was beaming, looking proud of herself despite her bright pink blush. "You're so damn cute."

She giggled. "And you're so damn handsome."

He smiled. "Breathtaking?"

She bit her lip, nodding and smiling.

He shook his head, still smiling. Sweet and sexy. He hit the accelerator.

"What would you do if you had all the time and money in the world?" she asked.

He thought about that. "I'd build you the house of your dreams."

"Get out! You would not."

"I would."

"This is supposed to be about you."

"I like building stuff. And I like making you happy."

She sniffled. He glanced over to find her digging a tissue out of her tiny purse and wiping under her eyes. "You're crying?" he asked. "Geez, I lost my touch."

"No, you've got it just fine."

"Okay, tell me about you. Answer all the same questions."

She looked up before turning back to him. "My life is so boring. I grew up in a middle-class suburb of Connecticut, went to college, got pregnant, dropped out and spent the next several years taking care of kids and the house. I'm terrible at sports. I used to love dance, in fact, I was a pretty good ballerina, but my legs and arms weren't long enough for the ideal. I was always in the background, never the principal dancer."

"You were part of the team."

She laughed. "In a way, I guess. I get along with my parents okay. I have a younger sister who lives in Rhode Island. She's a jewelry designer."

"So artists run in your family."

"I never thought about it like that before. I guess so. And if I had all the time and money in the world, I would just create art all day long." She paused. "Sorry, mine's a lot more selfish than yours."

"Building stuff makes me happy, creating stuff makes you happy. We're alike that way. It's not selfish to do what you love."

She sighed.

"What's that sigh about?" he asked. Sometimes a woman's sigh could have all sorts of hidden meanings.

She sat straighter. "I just really, really like you."

He took her hand and gave it a squeeze. "Me too. Like you, that is."

They exchanged a quick smile, and he knew this date was going to go great.

How such a macho-looking, manly man like Vinny could be such a sweetheart astounded her. But he was. He held doors open for her, pulled her chair out for her, and expressed himself so openly, so warmly. All of that and he was breathtakingly gorgeous, sexy too, though she wasn't ready to go there yet.

They'd both ordered the lobster, a special treat, and now their plates were just shells from their delicious meal.

"You want dessert?" he asked.

She shook her head. "I'm really full between the bread, the lobster, mashed potatoes, and vegetables. It was all so wonderful. Thanks for picking such a nice place."

"I figure you're used to nice places."

"Oh." Shit. Maybe he couldn't even afford this place. She didn't know how much he made, but he'd said he lived in a town that was going downhill, but he stayed because he could afford it. And they'd ordered the most expensive things on the menu. "I do like nice places, and this place is really nice...why don't we split the bill?"

"No way. I asked you to dinner, I'll pay."

She wasn't surprised at all. In some ways, he was very traditional, but not in a stuffy way. More like good manners and a strong sense of right and wrong. "Thank you."

He grunted, looking a little offended.

She tried to smooth things over. "I'm out of practice with dating. I thought people split the bill more nowadays." He gave her a skeptical look. "Anyway, for future dates, I mean, if you want to go on more dates—"

"You kidding me? Course I do."

"Okay, okay." She laughed a little because he looked so disgruntled. "For future, we don't always have to eat at a fancy place. I'm good with pizza, subs, burgers, whatever. I mean, that's what my kids like, so we have it regularly."

He took her hand and leaned close, his voice husky. "I wanted it to be special for you."

She melted. This man was nothing short of amazing. "It will be special as long as we're doing it together."

One corner of his mouth lifted, his dark eyes glinting with a mischievous look. She blushed, suddenly realizing what that sounded like—"doing it together." She really had to stop blushing like a schoolgirl every time she thought of getting physical with him. It was just that she was so out of practice.

He said nothing, only leaned back with a small smirk on his face.

"I'm out of practice with that too," she said.

He winked. "Like riding a bicycle."

Sure, if your bicycle was a massive hot rod between your legs. She felt herself flush again. *Don't think about it.*

"So damn cute," he said, getting a kick out of all her blushing.

"Once I'm back in the saddle, I swear I'll stop all this embarrassing blushing."

He smirked again, and she realized "back in the saddle" also sounded dirty. She waved that away. "You know what I mean. Dating is new."

He gave her a knowing look. "I get ya."

The undercurrent of sexual tension was new between

them and exciting. She wanted to match him but had no idea what to say back. "I get ya too."

He gave her a slow sexy smile that had her breath catching. "Ya know, that sounds real good."

Maybe she was good at this sexy flirting because there was definitely still a tension in the air. "It would be *real* good," she returned. Okay, so she was out of practice.

His expression was part amused, part intrigued.

The waiter arrived with the check, and Vinny quickly pulled out his wallet and handed over his credit card. Allie thanked Vinny before excusing herself to the ladies' room. Once there, she retouched her makeup and popped a breath mint in preparation for a goodnight kiss. And maybe more. Her belly dipped at the thought, but things just felt right with Vinny.

She returned to the table, catching Vinny carefully wiping his mouth with a napkin. Maybe he was making sure there was no leftover butter from the lobster in case they kissed. She smiled to herself and took a seat.

He held out his palm. "Mint? I had one. They're good."

She smiled. "Got one already."

He tore open the wrapper and popped it in his mouth.

Two minty mouths plus a kid-free night sounded very promising. She leaned across the table and gave him a brazen hint. "The kids are spending the night at my parents' place, so I have the house to myself."

His eyes were hot on hers. "You inviting me in?"

"Yes," she whispered.

He checked his watch and shook his head. "I don't have much time. My mother-in-law said I need to get the kids by nine. She needs her sleep; she has to take care of my father-in-law."

She pushed down her disappointment. It wasn't like she was going to sleep with him on their first date, but she'd hoped for a little intimacy, a tiptoe back into the lust pool. "How is he?"

"Surprisingly, he's hanging in there. I think being home

has been really good for him. Maybe he'll live longer than the doctors said. They only gave him a week."

"I hope so."

"Rain check?"

She tried to hide the disappointment from her voice. "Sure."

"I already paid. Ready?"

She nodded, and then they were on their way. So much buildup of nerves and anticipation for this date, and now it was almost over. She should be happy not disappointed. It was a good sign that she enjoyed his company so much that she didn't want it to end. There was absolutely no rush. They were getting to know each other, and that took time.

He took her hand, and the small gesture reminded her she could still look forward to a goodnight kiss. She quickly chewed her mint and swallowed, hoping it would give her maximum mintiness. They arrived at his car parked in the lot behind the restaurant. He opened her door and closed it behind her. She leaned her head back on the seat and sighed.

He got in, but he didn't start the car. "Allie."

She turned. "Yeah?"

His big hand cradling her jaw, he slowly leaned in, his gaze dropping from her eyes to her mouth. Her pulse beat rapidly, her body tingling in anticipation. His lips met hers in a soft kiss before he pulled back. "I've been wanting to do that all night."

"Do it again."

He did, grazing his lips over hers, once, twice, and she leaned in for more. He pulled back, dropping his hand from her face. His voice was husky. "We'd better go."

She faced front, embarrassed by how much more kissing she wanted when he was done. She glanced around. They were in a parking lot, other people coming out to their cars nearby. "Yes, of course."

He chuckled and started the car.

"What's so funny?" she asked.

"I like how you sound so pissy that we have to stop kissing. That means you want more."

"Maybe," she allowed.

"Definitely. You want me."

Now he was getting arrogant. "Maybe I do, maybe I don't."

"Uh-huh."

"Kiss me again if you want to find out."

He flashed a smile. "You bet I will."

She smiled to herself, pleased with his assurance.

"You want to go out again next Saturday night?" he asked.

"Yes," she replied immediately.

"That was a fast yes."

"I'm of an age where I know what I want," she said.

He smiled, his dark eyes sparkling with good humor. "I like the sound of that. See? There's benefits to dating at our age. We know what we want; we know when it's good." He took her hand and gave it a squeeze. "I'm lucky to have a second chance at dating with you."

"You're my second chance too. My first try was pretty bad."

"I'm sorry to hear it, but glad at the same time, ya know? Because now I get to be with you. You know what they say, second time's a charm."

"Is it? I thought it was third time."

His voice was warm and full of good humor. "Pretty sure it's second time."

He was joking, but she liked the sentiment. "You know, I think you might be right about that."

They drove back to her house, talking and laughing about the kids, hard not to when they were both single parents, but it was nice to share. He pulled into her driveway and shut off the car. For a moment, she thought they might have a makeout session in the car, but he got out, walked around and opened her car door.

"I was raised to walk my date to the front door," he said.

"Good with me." She got out and he took her hand, his larger hand enveloping hers in warmth, walking her to the front door. Both of them were quiet. Maybe he didn't want the night to end either.

She'd left the porch light on, and it occurred to her that her neighbors could witness a goodnight kiss. Screw it. That kiss was all she was getting tonight, and she wanted it much more than she cared about the gossips. She fished her key out of her purse and looked up at him. "Thanks for dinner. I had a wonderful time. So…goodnight."

He gazed at her for a moment, his eyes gleaming before he closed the distance between them, his hand cupping her jaw, tilting her head up, holding her as he kissed one corner of her mouth, then the other.

She gripped his shirt, pulling him in for more. And then it changed. His hand slid under her hair, cupping her head, as his mouth became more demanding, deepening the kiss, his tongue thrusting inside. Her stomach dipped, damp between the legs, and she threw her arms around his neck, returning the kiss passionately. His arm banded around her waist, half lifting her as his mouth plundered. She'd never been kissed like this before and she loved it. She ventured to taste, sliding her tongue along his, and he jerked back, breathing hard.

"Yeah," he said. "Time to go."

"Did I do something wrong?" she asked, mortified.

He groaned. "No, sweetheart, you do everything too good. Know what I'm sayin'?"

"I'm slutty?"

He barked out a laugh, then held her by the chin and gave her a quick kiss. "I'm saying I need to control myself because you are one sexy woman."

She smiled. "You're a good kisser."

He ran his thumb over her bottom lip. "I'm good at a lot of things."

There it was, that sexual-banter thing. She had to say something good in return to keep up with him. "I'm good at blowjobs."

He swore, pulled her close and kissed the top of her head. "Goodnight."

He turned and jogged down the porch steps.

"Was that too slutty?" she called after him.

He turned. "That was perfect." He blew her a kiss.

She caught it and put it to her lips. He put both hands to his heart, staggering a bit in an exaggerated gesture of *you got me* before heading off into the night.

She let herself back into the house and laughed a happy giddy laugh.

7

———

Allie drove to the city on Sunday afternoon to pick up her boys at their dad's apartment in a dreamy state. She'd been dating Vinny for two months now and was falling fast. It was like her whole life she'd been waiting for Vinny, and now that she'd finally found him, she wanted to see him all the time. Unfortunately, they'd only managed five dates in those two months. So many things went wrong, resulting in cancelling on each other. The babysitter fell through, or one of the kids was down with a stomach virus, or, sadly, his father-in-law passed. They had long phone conversations on those missed-date nights, sometimes talking for hours. They'd kept their kids out of their relationship. She hadn't even told her boys she was dating again, but lately she'd started to wonder if she should let them know. She felt that strongly about Vinny.

She'd missed a date with him this weekend because Angel had a high fever and Vinny understandably wanted to stay home and care for him. Too bad because she'd had the whole weekend free, no need for a babysitter when her boys were at their dad's place.

She parked in the apartment building's underground garage, rode the elevator to the lobby, and announced herself to the security guard at the front desk. After the guard checked in with William by phone, she was directed to the elevator and rode it to his luxury apartment.

The moment the apartment door opened, her chest clutched. William looked agitated, his expression pinched, his blue eyes steely. "What's wrong?" she asked.

"We need to talk about your sons," he said ominously.

"Our sons," she corrected.

"Hi, Mom," Gabe said, appearing next to his dad, looking perfectly fine. "We're all packed and ready to go."

"Just a moment. I need to talk to your dad."

Gabe's eyes darted to the side. "I can explain."

Uh-oh. "Later," she told him.

William stepped out into the hallway with her, shutting the door behind him. "Your sons are running wild. They weren't like this before. What's going on at home?"

She tensed. Wasn't that just like William to put all the blame at her feet? "Exactly how are they running wild?"

William looked down his nose at her. "Jared set a fire in my kitchen."

She gasped. Jared was seven. "Where'd he get the matches?"

"He found some in the kitchen drawer." He lifted a finger, smiling in a smug way like he enjoyed telling her how bad "her" sons were. "Then while I was putting that out, Luke stole the cash from my wallet—two hundred dollars—and the three of them bolted out of the apartment. They were gone for two hours this morning, running around the city."

Her heart lodged in her throat. Her three boys—seven, nine, and thirteen years old—running around New York City by themselves? "Why didn't you call me? Did you look for them? Did you have to get the police involved?"

"Of course I looked for them. The police wouldn't get involved since it had only been a short time. And I didn't call you because there was nothing you could do but freak out just like you're doing right now."

"Damn right I'm freaking out! They're too young to be running around by themselves. I can't believe this."

"I don't know what's come over them, but if this is the

way they're going to act, I'm not sure I want them to be guests in my home."

"Jesus, William! They're not guests! They're your children. I will talk to them and ensure this doesn't happen again, but you will be part of their lives. They need to know their dad."

He shook his head, his lips pressed together. "Are they acting like this at home?"

"No, they've been fine. Maybe the divorce has shaken them up more than I realized. It's a new thing for them, visiting you in a different place."

"It's been two months, and they get worse with every visit."

"What else have they done?"

He ran a hand through his thinning light brown hair. "This was definitely the worst of it, but they give me a lot of attitude. I don't think they want to be here."

"I'll talk to them."

He nodded once, turned, and opened the door, holding it for her.

The moment she walked in, her boys rushed at her, hugging her.

"Got our stuff!" Jared said, grabbing his backpack.

"Bye, Dad!" Luke said, rushing out the door.

"Bye," Gabe said to his dad sullenly. He probably knew better than the younger two that they were in big trouble.

She waited until they were out of the city, where she could focus on them better, and they were all trapped in the car so they'd have to listen to her. She turned off the radio. "Boys, your dad told me a hair-raising story of your visit this weekend, and I'm not at all happy."

"Sorry, Mom," Gabe said from the passenger seat next to her. The other two quickly chimed in from the backseat with their sorrys.

"Is it true?" she asked. "Jared, you set a fire, Luke, you stole money, and the three of you ran around like hoodlums in the city?"

"What's a hoodlum?" Jared asked.

"Shut up, idiot," Gabe said. "Mom, I kept a close eye on

them the whole time and got them back to dad's apartment no harm done. I memorized the map of the city."

She ground her teeth. Gabe at thirteen sounded a little too proud of his supervisory role. He should know better than to run away like that without permission. "I just can't understand why you would act this way. Were you mad at your dad?"

Silence.

"I want answers, you hear me?" she barked. "Jared, why did you start a fire?"

"Distraction," he said.

"Distraction for what?" she asked. It was like pulling teeth, but she'd get to the bottom of it. "Jared, answer me right now."

"Luke told me to make a distraction so he could get the money."

"I didn't say start a fire!" Luke snapped.

"Ow!" Jared exclaimed. "He hit me!"

A rustling and grunts started up in the backseat as the two boys smacked each other around.

"Knock it off!" she hollered at the top of her lungs.

Silence.

She took a deep calming breath. "Luke, why would you steal money?"

Luke responded like it was the most obvious thing in the world. "If we didn't have money, we couldn't ride the subway. And we definitely had to buy hot dogs from the sidewalk cart. Dad never lets us and they smell so good."

"I still don't understand," she said, barely hanging on to her patience. "Why did you have to run out of his apartment in the first place?"

"We didn't like the lady," Jared said.

She looked in the rearview mirror at her youngest boys and glanced over at Gabe, all three of them screwing up their faces in disgust. She swallowed hard. William must've wanted to introduce his girlfriend (or mistress) to the boys. He might've mentioned that glaring fact to her, or better yet, given her a heads-up so she could prepare the boys. Clearly the kids weren't ready to think of their dad dating someone that wasn't their mom.

"Boys, your dad and I are divorced now. He's single and free to date another woman. I want him to be happy."

"She reeks of flowers," Luke said.

"She called me a cute little boy," Jared said. "I'm not little!"

She looked to Gabe. "Who was this woman?"

"Dad said she was his friend, but we all saw her kiss him on the mouth." Someone made a retching sound from the backseat. "And he was so busy talking to her, we didn't think he'd even miss us."

She took a deep breath. "Okay, first of all, your behavior this weekend is unacceptable both to me and your dad. You'll be writing him a letter apologizing. I expect you to act just like you would at home when you're at his apartment. You all know the rules."

"Are we grounded?" Gabe asked.

She ignored that because she needed to make her point before they all moaned and groaned about their punishment. "I'm okay with your dad dating, and I hope he would be okay with me dating too."

"Does this mean you and Dad are never getting back together?" Gabe asked.

She glanced over at him, surprised. "Is that what you guys hoped?"

No answer.

"The divorce is final," she said. "When two people agree to legally end the marriage, that means they're not getting back together."

"Sometimes they do," Gabe said. "I saw it in a movie."

"Yeah," Luke and Jared chimed in.

Allie shook her head. "Not this time. Listen, I don't want you to be mad at your dad. This divorce was something we both wanted. We're happier now and are moving on with our lives. It was nobody's fault." Her throat tightened with all she felt for them. "You boys will always be just as loved by both of us."

The boys were quiet.

She needed to tell them about her dating, to prepare them a little, even if they didn't actually meet Vinny. "I've also recently started dating a very nice man. His name is Vinny, and I hope one day soon you'll get to meet him."

"We already got a dad," Luke said belligerently.

"And he will never replace your dad," she responded patiently. "I just want you boys to understand how both me and your dad are moving forward with other people, but like I said, that doesn't change how we feel about you. I love you guys. You'll always be the most important people in my life."

"Love you too," Gabe mumbled.

"I love you, Mommy," Jared said, sounding like his sweet little-boy self again.

Her heart squeezed.

"I love you too," Luke grumbled. "Just don't go marrying some stranger."

"No plans for that," she said. "We're still getting to know each other."

She waited, prepared to reassure them about whatever they might be worried about or answer any questions, but it seemed like the dating conversation was over. "Jared, we're going to be talking about fire safety when we get home."

"I know it," he replied cheerfully. "I visited the firehouse on a field trip. Stop, drop, and roll."

She gritted her teeth. "We're still going to talk. What you did was very dangerous. Got it?"

"Okay," he said.

She blew out a breath. "Okay, now that we cleared that up, you're all grounded for two weeks. And no video games for a month."

The car exploded with protests. Video games were their favorite.

She turned the radio back on, tuning them out.

～

Later that night, after the boys were in bed, and after an exhausting talk about fire safety with Jared, she collapsed on the living room sofa. She'd definitely have to follow up with Jared. His initial defense, "I wasn't *playing* with matches, I was *using* them," did not fly. She still wasn't convinced he understood just how dangerous the situation could've been. She thought about a glass of wine, but then she thought calling Vinny would be even better. Even when he spoke plainly or laced his speech with colorful swear words, she loved to hear his deep melodious voice in her ear.

She grabbed the phone and called him. "Hey, it's me. How's Angel doing?" She remembered he'd been sick.

"His fever finally broke," Vinny told her. "He's sleeping now. Poor kid. I can only talk for a bit because I got to get the Lysol out. Last thing I want is for the other two to get it."

"Yup, been there."

"I'm sorry we had to miss our date again this weekend."

She sighed. "Me too. If it's not one thing, it's another. I guess between us we've got six people to work around."

"Yeah."

She frowned. It sucked that she'd finally found someone she was crazy about, yet she hardly got to see him. And they hadn't had enough alone time to get intimate either. His kisses made her crave so much more. She was beginning to feel desperate.

Then he asked the one question guaranteed to cool her lust. "What if we start spending time together with the kids? Then we don't have to work around them."

After the harrowing ordeal with her boys today, she knew that was out of the question. "My kids aren't ready for that."

"How do you know? Maybe they'll have fun hanging out with my kids. They're all pretty close in age."

"The divorce just went through, and they've been acting out with their dad."

"Nip that behavior in the bud. They have to show respect."

And that respect needed to be earned. William didn't show a lot of love, and her boys felt that lack. Still, she knew the kids had to act much more responsibly. "I did, but still. It's too soon for them."

"Your divorce was two months ago. And he moved out months before that. I'm just saying—"

"No."

"Okay, just an idea."

She let out a breath, reaching for calm. No one, not even Vinny, could get between her and her kids. She knew what was best for them, and she absolutely knew they weren't ready to meet him. She had to take it slow; they'd only just found out today that she was dating again.

"I miss you," Vinny said.

She melted. He spoke openly from the heart and it got her every time. "I miss you too, so much."

"How about you and I go someplace just the two of us, check into a hotel for the weekend?"

Pure adrenaline shot through her, half excited, half nervous. It was what she'd been hoping for, but she'd be lying if she said it would be easy for her. It had been so very long. She lowered her voice. "Is hotel code for sex?"

He laughed. He got a real kick out of her speaking frankly. It was still new for her, but she liked it too. "We'll do what-ever feels comfortable for both of us, okay? If that's just watching a TV show for people above twelve years old with some frigging peace and quiet, I'd like that too."

She laughed.

"As long as I'm with you," he added.

She wanted to reach through the phone, wrap her arms around him, and hug him. How could she resist his invita-tion? She missed him so very much. "We could watch TV and have a picnic. Raid the minibar."

"That's cool with me too."

"Minibar could get expensive," she said.

"So we'll bring our own stuff for a picnic. Whatever you like."

She smiled. "It feels like it should be champagne. A cele-bration."

"Absolutely. Ya know, I was so tired when I got on the phone, but now I'm energized. This'll be good."

"How's next weekend?" she asked. "I'll see if my parents can stay with them."

"I'll check if my mother-in-law can stay the weekend here and let you know tomorrow."

She held the phone closer, smiling so big her cheeks hurt. "Perfect."

"I'll make the hotel reservations."

"We'll split the cost, okay?" She was doing just fine with alimony, child support, and her own money from her picture-book illustrations. William had done right by her and the boys, though her lawyer said she could've gotten a lot more. She'd let it slide, not wanting to drag out the divorce or cause any more acrimony between them. After all, she still had to see him regularly because of the boys.

"When ya gonna get it?" Vinny huffed. "I invite, I pay."

"Okay, but next time I'm inviting you to something and I'm paying."

"Gotta be quicker, then."

She heard a little-boy voice in the background.

"Gotta go. Angel's up and needs a glass of water. Talk to you tomorrow." He hung up.

She hung up too, staring at nothing. Had she really just agreed to shack up in a hotel with Vinny? It sounded so sordid, so unlike her. Would sex ruin what they had? What if they weren't compatible? Or what if they were? This could catapult them to a whole new level in their relationship. One that could involve the kids. And what kind of reaction would she get from her ex or, for Vinny, from his mother-in-law, who looked after Vinny and his family. She blew out a harsh breath. This could get real complicated real fast.

Maybe they'd just kick back, relax, and watch TV with their picnic. Do a little sightseeing.

She stood on shaky legs, her body knowing what her mind was having trouble accepting, it was time to get back on that horse. Except her horse was a massively large stallion.

~

Vinny drove to Allie's house the following Friday night pumped for a whole weekend together. This was definitely a step forward in their relationship. He could hardly believe they'd pulled it off with the six kids all staying healthy, no major catastrophes. All of them well cared for and accounted for. His mother-in-law had agreed to watch the boys, and he knew it was mostly because she needed the distraction after her husband's passing. Of course, it hadn't been that easy. Loretta had given him the third degree about Allie, agreeing to babysit on the condition that she meet her formally for Sunday dinner to see "what this woman was made of." Whatever that meant. He'd agreed, sorta. He would've said anything to get this weekend with Allie.

Was he looking forward to sex? Absolutely. He already knew they'd be compatible. Their kisses told him everything. Passion was there all right. She was sexy as all hell and he wanted her so badly it hurt. It was so hard to leave her at the end of their dates. Finally he wouldn't have to. This could only bring them closer. Of course, that would come with different complications. They were both a package deal with the kids and his mother-in-law and…aw, hell. He didn't want to think about all that. He just wanted to enjoy this rare weekend away with her.

Only the moment she stepped out of her house, dragging a large wheeled suitcase behind her, he knew she wasn't on the same page. Her entire body radiated tension, her expression pinched.

"Here, lemme get your suitcase," he said, reaching for it.

"No problem," she said tersely. "It's on wheels. I've got it."

He walked with her to his car, loaded her suitcase in the back alongside his duffel bag, and got in the driver's seat. He turned to her. "Everything okay with the kids?"

She smiled tightly. "They're fine."

He tried again, hoping she'd relax now that they were about to have a great weekend. No kids, no worries. "The hotel's supposed to be a nice place, up north to Mystic, Connecticut, by the beach."

"Maybe tomorrow we could explore the Mystic Seaport," she said with zero enthusiasm.

"Sure. Unless we're busy." He caught her eye and winked.

She smoothed her hair, her movements jerky.

Oh-kay. He pulled out of the driveway and headed through town. She remained stiff and quiet. He tried a few surefire conversation starters: What's new? How's your painting going? What'd you pack for the picnic? All of which she answered in as few words as possible in the most uptight voice he'd ever heard come out of her.

He gave up and stopped talking, putting the radio on instead.

She stared out the window, saying nothing for miles and miles and miles.

Now he was getting tense. He'd been looking forward to this all frigging week, especially after the rough weekend he'd had getting up a bunch of times in the night to take care of Angel. "What's wrong?" he asked.

"Nothing."

"Don't tell me nothing. Something's wrong. Just spit it out."

She scowled. "Don't tell me what to do."

He tamped down his temper, trying for a calm voice. "Allie, I was so looking forward to this. You know the last time I got a weekend off from parenting? Never. Not once. It's all me, all the time." He took a deep breath, working for patience. "And I get to spend it with you. I thought you were excited too, but all I'm getting from you is tension. Now I ask you again, what's wrong?"

"Nothing, I just..." She coughed. "It's just that I'm a little...worked up."

Finally. Something he could work with. "Worked up about what?"

"Shit. I feel like a complete idiot even mentioning it."

The fact that she cursed meant it was serious. "Tell me," he ordered.

"It's just that I've been thinking about you and me together, and then I started worrying…" She trailed off and he waited.

A long tense moment passed with no further explanation.

"What're you worried about?" he asked with his last shred of patience.

"Are you big everywhere?"

He grinned, thrilled she was exactly on the same page as he was, thinking about his cock. "Whaddya think you get this big hunk of man with a tiny package?"

She fidgeted in her seat. "I don't know."

He winked. "Let's just say you won't be disappointed."

"Oh." She stared out the windshield, and he caught a bright pink blush on her cheeks in the streetlight glow.

"What's the problem?"

She faced him. "I'm petite and it's been *years* for me."

He reached over and squeezed her hand. "I think you can manage me."

Her voice was high and reedy. "My boys were C-sections, so everything's pretty tight, if you know what I mean."

Oh-kay. "Sounds good to me."

"I have a nasty scar on my stomach. Fair warning."

"We all have scars, whether or not they show."

"Anything you want to warn me about?" she asked.

He passed a slow car and hit the accelerator, eager to get to the hotel. "Like what?"

"I don't know!"

"Few scars from football and work. Nothing to write home about. I'm just flesh and bones, same as you."

"You're much, much bigger than me."

"Trust me, it's not gonna be a problem." He glanced over at her, tense as all hell again. She was so worried about him being big and her being little and tight. Damn, that made him hot just thinking about their joining, so he spoke plainly, directly addressing her sexy concern. "I'll get you nice and hot and wet, and then I'll just slide in there."

"Vinny!" Her hands fluttered in the air, her face bright red.

He backpedaled. "That wasn't very romantic, right?" He

scrambled for something good. "We'll just do whatever feels right. You tell me if you want me to, ya know, take a hike, take a cold shower. Whatever."

She stilled. "And you wouldn't be mad?"

"Nah, not mad." *Disappointed as fuck, but…*

"Okay." She gripped her hands tightly together in her lap and stared at them.

This was going to be a long night.

He hadn't expected her to be so tense. He'd thought they were pretty comfortable with each other.

"This is my first time in years too," he said in a teasing voice. "Be gentle with me."

She laughed a little, still tense.

All right, this was ridiculous. He was not going to pussy-foot around her nerves. TV could wait, picnic could wait. He was going full steam ahead the moment they walked into that hotel room. The more they postponed the inevitable, the more worked up she'd get. They'd said all that needed to be said.

It was going to be down and dirty.

He suspected that was exactly what she needed.

8

———

Ally waited for Vinny to check them in, pacing the hotel foyer and wondering what the hell was wrong with her. Why couldn't she relax? Just because she hadn't been with a man in years. She and William had stopped having sex years before the divorce. She hadn't cared at the time; now she did because this time with Vinny felt like much more of a big deal than she wanted it to be. The more she told herself to relax, the more nervous she got. And Vinny, he was a big man. Big, big, big. And she was not at all.

And she was so out of practice and her scar had repulsed William and Vinny was acting like this was no big deal at all!

He crossed to her, plastic key card in hand, a small duffel bag over his shoulder. She had a large wheeled suitcase because she couldn't decide on clothes or shoes. She'd also tucked a plastic bag with a can of mixed nuts, snack-sized bags of potato chips, and a pack of Oreos for their picnic in her suitcase. Basic minibar stuff at a much cheaper price. She focused on that. A fun picnic was much easier to think about than sex.

"All set," he said. "Two nights."

She shouldn't have agreed to the entire weekend. One night would've been plenty. What if they were completely incompatible in bed? What were they going to do the second night?

She lagged behind him on the way to the elevator. He was whistling a cheerful tune. She wanted to smack him. How dare he act so happy when he should be just as worked up as she was. This was a big deal. The first time for both of them in years. Only the second man she'd ever been with, and he'd said she was the second woman for him.

This was a HUGE deal!

She stepped into the elevator with him along with a couple of other people. She stared straight ahead.

"We're fourth floor," Vinny told her.

"Mmm-hmm."

There were five floors. They reached the fourth, and she stepped out first, waiting for him. He held up the key card and gestured in the direction of the room.

"Nice place," he said as they walked down the thick carpet. "We have a balcony with a view of the garden."

"Yup," she said, her lips popping with the sound. Weird. She could barely feel her lips.

He stopped at their hotel door, opened it and took her suitcase from her, bringing their stuff inside. She took a deep breath and followed him in. His broad back was to her as he set the luggage on the far side of the room.

"Are you hungry?" she asked. Her appetite had fled the moment she'd packed her suitcase.

He turned, stalking toward her, towering over her, dark intent in his eyes.

She gulped, backing up a step. "Vinny?"

He didn't reply, stopping in front of her, his gaze colliding with hers for one hot moment before his arm banded around her waist, pressing her tight against him, his lips crashing down on hers. A hot rush of desire shot through her. His big hand cupped the back of her head, and then he was backing her up against the wall, his mouth hard and demanding, lifting her leg and grinding against her as he plundered her mouth. She ignited, a low moan ripped from her throat, lifting her hips to meet him.

His hands were everywhere at once, cupping her breasts, down her sides, her bottom, never breaking the connection, his mouth devouring hers, and then he lifted her, shifting himself firmly between her legs, and she wrapped her arms and legs around his big body. He ground into her again and hit just the right spot. Her head dropped back, and his mouth went to her neck, his teeth scraping against her. She'd never felt like this before, sensations flooding her, her mind clouded. He sucked on her neck, hard, as he ground against her over and over, the intensity too much, hot and tight. She exploded with a sharp cry, stunned by the rush of it, and then all of her relaxed.

He lifted his head and grinned. "Nice." He set her on her feet and steadied her for a moment before he stroked a finger down the side of her neck. "You're gonna have a hickey."

"My first."

He flashed a wolfish smile and then yanked off her shirt. His fingers sure and superfast, the bra went next, then her pants. She was too relaxed to care, her eyes nearly closed, drenched in a pleasure far too long denied. Her panties went down next.

He ran his hands down her sides. "Beautiful."

She looked up at him, all tension gone. "Make love to me."

His hand slid between her legs, and her knees buckled. He spoke against her lips. "That's the plan."

She pulled at his shirt and he stepped back, pulling it off himself. She gazed in awe at his massive muscles, all from physical labor, not sculpted at the gym. From the bulge of his shoulders and biceps to his chest with some dark hair leading down his flat stomach to another bulge in his jeans.

She reached for the button on his jeans. "Take it all off."

He held her hands in his and gave her a sexy smile. "Not yet. I want to get you off."

"You did."

He leaned close, his hand slipping between her legs again. "And I want to do it again."

She nodded, beyond speech as he stroked her, guiding her back to lean against the wall, his body close enough to feel his heat. He crowded her, but she didn't feel trapped or too small. She felt glorious, her fingers running through his soft hair. He watched her as he stroked her, learning her by touch. The sensations were like a drug, and she closed her eyes, letting him do as he pleased.

His hand held her jaw, tipping her face up for his kiss. She wrapped both arms around his neck, throwing herself into the kiss with wild abandon. Lips and teeth and tongue, all of it fierce and hot, setting her on fire. He slid thick fingers inside her, and she gasped into his mouth. He shifted his hand, his fingers deep inside her, his calloused thumb stroking back and forth over pleasure central, making her body jerk with the sharp sensations. She tore her mouth away.

He kept stroking, his fingers thrusting slow and deep, making her ache. Hot, she was so hot. His mouth returned to her neck, nipping her. She jolted, her fingernails digging into his shoulders, and he nipped her again, his fingers stretching inside her. She whimpered, the ache too much, and then he was stroking her faster and faster, and the ache faded, all of her coiled and tight. Oh, God, she couldn't take much more. He kissed her again, thrusting inside her, stroking her, over-whelming her. She cried out, the sound swallowed by his mouth, and came hard, her ears ringing, light headed with it.

He broke the kiss and she panted, trying to catch her breath. His fingers still held her captive, and she throbbed against him. Their gazes collided, and he slid his fingers from her, put one long finger in his mouth, and sucked. She throbbed at the erotic gesture, pulsing with need.

He gave her a wicked smile, his voice deep and rough, scraping against her insides. "Nice and hot and wet. Now I can just slide in there."

This time the words didn't intimidate her, they drew her in, her hands reaching up to frame his gorgeous face before kissing him passionately, her hands wandering over all his warm hard muscle, wanting nothing more than their joining. He picked her up, cradled in his arms, and carried her toward the bed.

"Vinny?"

"Yeah." His voice was husky and so sexy.

Okay, this was going to be awkward, but she was a modern woman who could speak openly about these things. "Do you want more kids? I thought we should talk about that."

He halted halfway to the bed, staring down at her in his arms. "Do you mean do I want to meet yours or the brand-new kind?" His voice came out in a croak. "Babies?"

"Yes, babies."

He winced. "I don't think I could do the baby thing again."

She laughed a little. "I'm trying to have a talk about birth control. I brought condoms."

His eyes widened. "You did?"

"Yes," she said primly. "Why do you sound so surprised?"

"I thought that was my responsibility since I'm the one wearing them."

"Oh. So you brought them too?"

"Yeah." He continued walking to the bed.

"I wish I'd known," she said. "I drove half an hour away to buy them so I wouldn't run into anyone I know."

They laughed.

He pulled back the covers and gently set her down. "We good now?"

"How many did you buy?"

"I dunno. A box. I guess twelve in there."

"I bought twelve too."

He blew out an exaggerated breath. "Boy, that's a tall order, but I'll try." She must've looked as shocked as she felt because then he added, "Kidding!"

He stripped out of his jeans and joined her in the bed, kissing her breathless until she was crazed with need, grabbing his shoulders, pulling him close, eager to join with him. He broke the kiss, ran his thumb over her lower lip and pressed on it, his gaze locked on hers for one sizzling moment. But then instead of kissing her again, he got out of bed. She waited for him to strip out of his boxer briefs, but he turned and walked away.

"Hey!" she protested. "Get back here and finish what you started."

"Bossy woman," he teased. "I'm getting a condom."

"Hurry up!"

He groaned. "First she's afraid to be with me; now she's ordering me to fuck her."

"F-u-u-uck me."

"The mouth on you." She could hear the smile in his voice as he dug through his duffel bag. He quickly stripped, his back to her, and she checked him out. Even his ass was muscled, leading to strong muscled legs. Forget Michelangelo's *David*, they should make a marble statue of Vinny. He was that beautifully formed.

Finally he turned and strode toward her. "I fucking love it." Her breath caught at his erection, thick and long. He joined her in the bed, pulling her so they were side by side, stroking down her side as he kissed her.

She grabbed his ass and pulled him tight against her, determined to see this through no matter what. His leg wedged between hers, applying delicious pressure. She shifted to whisper in his ear, "I'm ready. Let's do this."

He rolled on top of her, fitting himself between her legs. "You ready, huh? Think you can handle me?"

She swallowed. "I think."

"Don't think, love." He kissed her tenderly as he slowly pushed inside her, her mind latching onto the sweet term of endearment, *love*, even as she ached, stretching to accommodate his size.

He gazed into her eyes as he pushed deeper. "You okay?"

"Are you all the way in?" she managed.

He stilled. "You can't tell?"

"It's a lot, it's a lot."

He kissed her, rocking against her, easing in at the same time as he brought her pleasure. She could feel her body tightening with another release even as he pushed her open.

She broke the kiss, half out of her mind, needing relief from the pressure, from the tension.

She tried to tell him what she needed. "Just, please, just...ah."

His mouth covered hers, and then he was fully inside, filling her to her womb. She gasped into his mouth and he shifted, kissing her temple, then her cheek, trailing to her ear. "We fit," he rasped in her ear. "You're so tight I feel like I'm gonna die happy."

She whimpered incoherently, needing release, needing the ache to fade to get there, needing him to *do something*.

He shifted to kiss her and grinned. "You feel amazing."

"Please," she gasped out, not even sure what she needed, but it was *something*.

"Wrap your legs around me."

She did.

"Now breathe."

She'd been holding her breath. She took a deep breath and nodded. His hand slipped under her hip and tilted her up as he thrust slow and deep, pleasure radiating through her, the ache fading. "Yes-s-s," she hissed out on a long breath.

"Yes," he said, his gaze locked on hers. "Yes."

She couldn't look away, his dark eyes heated, his features in the throes of passion amping up her own pleasure. To know she did that to him, her body with its scar that he hadn't even looked twice at, her out-of-practice petite self brought this gorgeous big man pleasure. He nipped her bottom lip and then sucked it, his thrusts deep, rocking her, possessing her.

He lifted his head, thrusting faster, his expression fierce, rocking, rocking, rocking. She exploded, a sharp cry ripped from her throat, and then he was thrusting through her release, bringing waves of pleasure through her body. He groaned, shuddering against her with his own release.

He gave her some of his weight, still holding himself up on his forearms. Even in the aftermath, he was thoughtful enough not to crush her with his weight. That was new for her. Everything about making love with Vinny was a new and amazing experience for her.

He rolled off her and lay on his back, breathing hard.

"You're so wonderful," she blurted.

He grabbed her hand and squeezed. "Thanks, you too." A few moments passed before he added, "You're gonna be sore. Tomorrow I'll go easy on you. Sunday we'll experiment."

She gulped. "Experiment?"

"Yeah."

"What does that mean?"

He waved a hand lazily in the air. "I'll maneuver you into a few different positions, see which ones you can take me in without gasping in shock."

She was already gasping in shock. "What positions?"

"I dunno. I'll move you around, see what works."

"Move me around," she echoed. "Like a doll."

He rolled to his side and kissed her. "Like a lover. You'll like it."

"That's how it's gonna be, huh?"

He shifted, lying flat on his back again. "That's how it's gonna be. And I won't hear any complaints tomorrow, that's for sure."

"And why is that?"

"Because your legs will be around my ears."

She throbbed at the thought, hot all over. How could he do that so easily? She propped up on an elbow to look at him. His eyes were closed, his thick lashes fanned out on his cheeks, a small smile on his full lips. She adored this man.

She kissed him. "Dirty, dirty mouth."

"Ha. You like it."

"I love it." *And I love you.* The thought scared her. Because where did they go from here? Mixing together six kids, forcing them to become a family when their own families had fallen apart. She knew her kids couldn't handle it. Vinny's kids might even resent her trying to take their mother's place. Not that she ever could, but kids viewed the world differently than an adult.

Not for the first time she wished she'd met Vinny under different circumstances.

He got out of bed, magnificently naked, heading to the bathroom. He returned a few minutes later, turned off the light, and slid into bed with her. "Night."

It was the first time they'd ever said goodnight and actually spent the night together. "Night," she whispered, rolling to her side, her usual sleeping position.

He wrapped an arm around her and spooned her from behind, heating her entire body.

"You ever think about the future?" she whispered.

"Try not to."

"Why?"

"Because I worry about the kids."

Boy, did she get that. Easier to take it one day at a time. One crisis at a time. She fidgeted a bit, not used to sleeping with a man.

He put a hand to her head, stilling her. "Sleep. You'll need your energy to take me on tomorrow." He was teasing with his sexy banter.

"I thought you were going easy on me tomorrow."

He sank his teeth into the side of her neck and she gasped. His voice was velvet. "I'll be going easy; you'll be coming hard over and over and over."

Electrified, she lay in the dark, eyes wide open, imagining all he'd promised. She had no doubt he'd follow through magnificently. Compatibility? Check. Future? Big old question mark.

9

Allie was in love, truly in love for the first time in her life. She never thought, as a single mom in her thirties, it would happen for her, but by some miracle, there it was. Four months of dating and she was dizzy with all that she felt for Vinny. She hadn't told him of her love, and he hadn't said the words either. She figured neither of them was ready to cross that line and what it meant for their future because it would be complicated. It was a matter of time, the *right* time, before she took things to the next level with Vinny once she knew her boys could handle it. As it was, the boys were still giving their dad attitude, despite repeated talks from her and revoking of video game privileges (their favorite thing). William had to be the one to step up, but he didn't want to punish them, saying they didn't like visiting him as it was, and he didn't want to make it worse. When her boys finally calmed down, it would mean they had accepted the divorce situation.

Another real concern, once the boys were brought into it, actually meeting Vinny as her serious boyfriend, she knew they'd blab to their dad. She worried her ex would be vindictive, making things difficult for her either with the boys or with money. It was one thing for him to date, but he'd never much liked her seeking her own happiness. Jerk.

And what would Vinny expect of her if they took things to the next level? Would he want her to move in? Take care of his kids along with hers? She wasn't sure she was ready to be a mom to six kids.

Vinny kept inviting her and the boys to do things with his family, which was good because she knew he must be serious about her, but also bad because she had to keep turning him down. He kept it casual, low-key. Like when he invited them to join his family to see a movie or to join them for their town's Christmas tree lighting. And then, finally, just before the New Year, she was backed into a corner. It was inevitable after four months of dating, yet it had still taken her by surprise.

She'd had a late date with Vinny the night before, paying the babysitter extra so Allie could sneak home with him for some much-needed bedroom time after his babysitter left. She'd snuck out again after, his kids none the wiser. Now it was Sunday morning; she'd slept in and felt decadent. Sleeping with Vinny was truly a piece of heaven for her. She could hear the boys loudly playing their own version of Monopoly downstairs. Her phone rang and she quickly picked up.

"Good morning," Vinny's deep voice crooned, sounding a little smug because last night he'd made her come undone. She'd made sounds she'd never made in her life, primal animal sounds that he covered with his kisses, and then she'd collapsed, completely boneless. It had been so hard to leave his warm bed, but her responsibilities as a mom were never far from her mind.

"Morning," she replied cheerfully.

"I had a great time last night."

"Me too."

"Course, I always do with you, love."

She smiled the biggest goofiest smile on the planet. "You're so sweet."

He spoke earnestly. "You know I care about you. You're important to me."

"Yes," she said, suddenly wary.

"I'd really like you and your boys to come over tonight for Sunday dinner. I want my kids to get to know the woman I'm crazy about, and I want your kids to know me too. My mother-in-law would also really like to meet you."

Her heels dug in automatically. Vinny was for her, not her boys. Besides, it had only been four months since the divorce was official and the boys weren't ready. She spoke in a gentle tone, hoping to lessen the rejection. "I already planned dinner tonight. Their favorite—burgers."

"No," Vinny said.

"No?" she echoed, confused.

"Hold on." There was a rustling sound like he'd covered the phone. He spoke in a low tone to someone, and then he was back, his voice resigned. "Allie, Loretta would like to say hello."

And then a woman's voice got on the phone. "Hello, I'm Loretta, Vincent's mother-in-law."

The woman's tone was so authoritative Allie sat up straight in bed. "Hi, I'm Allie."

"Allie, I've heard a great deal about you and know you mean a lot to Vincent, so I'd like to formally invite you and your sons to Sunday dinner at my home."

"That's very nice of you, but—"

"Do you deny my request?"

Allie ran a hand through her hair. "I was just telling Vinny that—"

"Do you know what I have lost?" Loretta asked quietly.

Allie stilled, her chest tightening. Loretta had lost her daughter and recently her husband. Allie could only imagine the pain the woman had been through. "Yes, I know."

"Then you know Vinny and the boys are my world. Now you are in that world, and I would like to meet you. Is it too much to ask you to share one meal with me?"

"No, of course not."

"Good. It's settled. I'll see you at five p.m. sharp." She rattled off the address. "Hold on, I'll get Vinny."

There was another low conversation between Loretta and Vinny, and then Vinny was back. He kept his voice low.

"Allie, I don't want you to feel pressured. She said she just wanted to say hello. If you're not up for this, I'll tell her, okay?"

"I thought you threw me under the bus."

"I would never do that. Really. No pressure. She's just been asking about you. She's a force to be reckoned with, though she means well."

"Do you want me to go?"

"Very much. I feel good about where we're at."

She let out a shaky breath, reaching deep for what she wanted. And what she wanted more than anything was Vinny. "Me too. Okay, we'll be there."

"Thank you. I'm really looking forward to it."

She swallowed hard, not at all sure if she was ready for what this dinner would bring. It was so much more than just a dinner, this meeting of families, especially for her boys. "I need to go. See you later."

They said their goodbyes, and Allie disconnected with trembling hands. Now she had to explain to her boys not only that they'd be meeting the man in her life, but also other children, motherless children, who might also need her love. Would they be willing to share her? Could they accept actually seeing Mom with a boyfriend? All of the complications she'd feared fired through her brain—

Her boys adjusting to a man in her life that was not their dad.

Her ex's reaction.

His mother-in-law.

Vinny's expectations.

All those kids!

She girded her loins. First things first, she needed to talk to her boys.

Later that day, she made them burgers for lunch since they'd be having dinner tonight with the Marino family. They were so happy she almost felt guilty telling them the big news. She waited until they were nearly done eating before saying, "Boys, I have some news."

They all looked up at her curiously, still chewing.

She took a deep breath and pasted on a smile. "You know I've been dating Vinny for a while now, and he's invited all of us to dinner tonight."

Gabe stopped eating. "Is that why we got burgers for lunch?"

"Yes," she said.

Luke and Jared went back to their burgers.

She kept going. "And the nice thing is that he has three sons pretty close in age to you guys, so you'll have someone to play with."

Gabe frowned. "Mom, I'm thirteen. I don't play. I hang out."

"Sure, you can all hang out," she said, giving all three of them a big smile. "How's that sound?"

Luke spoke around his burger. "Are you gonna marry this guy?" This was the second time Luke had mentioned marriage.

It had crossed her mind, of course, but the idea of getting married again so soon after her divorce scared her. What if it didn't work out? She didn't think she could handle another divorce.

She exhaled sharply. "I don't know. I mean, not anytime soon." She cleared her throat. "That's not where we're at right now."

"Was that a yes or a no?" Gabe asked.

"No," she said.

"Good," Luke said, "'cuz we already have a dad." *Got it, Luke, no replacing your dad.*

"Are one of his kids my age?" Jared asked.

"Yes," she said, back on firm ground. Jared, despite being a daredevil, was the most easygoing of her sons. "His youngest, Angel, is seven too."

"Angel?" Jared asked, his nose crinkling. "That's a funny name."

"It's short for Angelo," she said.

Jared shrugged and took a big swallow of milk, leaving a milk mustache that he wiped away with his sleeve.

"Napkin," she said automatically.

The boys finished up in silence. Jared popped up from the table, and she grabbed him by the arm. "Wait. Does anyone have any questions about tonight?"

Gabe looked at her somberly. "Do we have to dress up?"

"No."

"Yay!" Jared cheered. "I hate dressing up." This one played hard; half the time he was covered in dirt.

"What're they having for dinner?" Luke asked.

"We'll have to wait and find out," she said.

"Can we go now?" Gabe asked.

She released Jared. "Yes."

The boys took off, and she sat at the quiet kitchen table, waiting for the other shoe to drop. That had been way too easy.

Allie arrived at Loretta's colonial home ten minutes early. She'd hustled the boys out with time to spare just so she'd get there on time. She'd baked some brownies for the kids to have for dessert and then merely prayed that her kids would behave themselves. They'd been unusually quiet on the drive over; even Jared had been quiet.

She gathered her boys close on the front porch. "Now remember your manners. Say please and thank you. Call Vinny, Mr. Marino, and call Loretta...shoot. I don't know her last name. Just wait and see how she introduces herself."

"We know, Mom," Gabe said on a long drone. Like she was the most irritating person on the planet.

"We always use our manners," Luke said. "Are you going to ring the bell?"

"Yes."

Jared jabbed it multiple times. She yanked his hand away. "Once is enough."

The door opened to an older Italian woman, wearing an apron, her gray hair in a bun. "Come in, welcome, I'm Mrs. Costa."

Allie ushered her boys inside, saying, "Thanks so much

for having us, Mrs. Costa." As if the woman hadn't twisted her arm with good old-fashioned guilt.

Allie glanced over at Vinny and his three boys standing to one side all in a row. Vinny gave her a wink and a smile. She smiled back, her heart warming for this wonderful man she loved so much. She instantly forgave the push that had gotten her here tonight. Without that push, she would've dragged her feet indefinitely. Her love for Vinny made this meeting inevitable.

She returned her attention to Mrs. Costa, who was studying her very closely. Allie tried not to squirm.

She offered the brownie tray to their host. "I made dessert."

Mrs. Costa took the brownies. "You cook?"

"Yes," she said. "Not an expert or anything, but gotta feed the kids. I'd be fine with salad or cereal."

Mrs. Costa arched a brow. "Vinny is an excellent cook. I taught him everything I know."

"That's wonderful," she said. She checked in with Vinny, a little surprised to hear he was *excellent* at cooking. He shrugged modestly. She hadn't had the experience of his cooking yet. Vinny always took her out. Maybe he wanted a break from the daily chore.

"Of course," Mrs. Costa said coolly. "He had to learn Italian cooking so his sons can have the cooking their mother would've provided." She turned and walked toward the kitchen.

Vinny closed the distance between them, leaning down to kiss her cheek and whisper in her ear, "How're you doing?"

"I'm fine." She took a step away, not sure if her boys would appreciate any public displays of affection.

Vinny turned to her boys. "Hello, I'm Vinny."

"Oh, yes," Allie said. "Vinny, this is Gabe."

Vinny shook his hand. "Nice to meet you."

"Nice to meet you, Mr. Marino," Gabe said in a subdued voice.

"This is Luke," she said.

Luke shook Vinny's hand. "Hi."

"Nice firm grip there," Vinny commented. He turned to Jared. "I remember you, Jared."

Jared beamed. "I remember you too! You let me use your hammer."

"What?" Allie exclaimed. "When did that happen?"

Vinny laughed. "You never asked your mom if it was okay, did you?"

Jared ran over to Angel and said something to him.

"I didn't know that," Allie said.

Vinny shrugged. "He came up to the art studio and said it was okay with you. I let him hammer in some sheetrock." He turned to his boys. "Come on over. She doesn't bite."

His boys walked over—Vince meeting her eyes warily, Nico looking curious, and Angel already smiling. Vince was the spitting image of his dad, already big at twelve. His face looked like it was stamped with his dad's exact features—dark eyes with thick lashes, high cheekbones, strong nose and jaw, full lips. Nico was also striking, his features quite refined, a softer version of his dad's, his manner reserved. Angel was simply adorable with rumpled dark hair and a dimpled smile.

Vinny introduced them, tapping them on the head as he did. "Vince, Nico, Angel, this is Ms. Reynolds."

"Nice to meet you," Vince and Nico mumbled in unison. Their dad had probably coached them.

"Hi!" Angel said. "Can Jared and I go back to my house? He wants to see my skateboard."

"No," Vinny said. "It's family time."

"But we'll be back before dinner," Angel said. "I know the way and I'll check the clock."

"Go show Jared the model train set in the basement," Vinny said.

"Okay," Angel said, as easygoing as Jared. "Come on, Jared."

They left.

The older boys eyed each other. Vinny herded them to the living room, where Gabe and Vince sat at opposite ends of the sofa. Nico and Luke sat on the floor, and Vinny took the recliner. She could sit on the floor or between Vince and Gabe. She took the middle seat on the sofa.

Vinny leaned forward, elbows on his knees, asking her boys how old they were, probably so his boys would know. He already knew a lot about them from her; they spoke of their kids often. Luke and Nico were the same age; Gabe was nearly two years older than Vince. Vinny moved onto sports talk, and Allie watched her boys carefully to see how they were taking things. Gabe was a little on edge but trying at least. Luke was giving one-word answers. Vince and Nico spoke easily and enthusiastically about their favorite teams. They were probably sweethearts just like their dad. It seemed like hours passed with Allie on the edge of her seat, not sure if she should intervene and tell Gabe to relax and Luke to stop with the monosyllables, when Loretta finally put an end to the awkwardness.

"Dinner!" Loretta caroled.

Vinny went to the basement door and called Jared and Angel to dinner. The rest of them gathered in a dining room set with nice china and cloth napkins. She wasn't sure if this was a typical Sunday dinner or if Loretta had tried to make it a special occasion. Two trays of manicotti took center stage, along with a big bowl of salad.

Loretta sat at the head of the table with Vinny taking a seat at the other end. Allie sat next to Vinny, and the kids filled in.

"Everything looks so nice, Loretta," Allie said.

"Thank you," Loretta said. "Would you like some wine?"

"No, thanks. I'm driving."

"Just a little, then," Loretta said, indicating the bottle of wine set on the nearby buffet.

"I'm good, but thanks."

Loretta sent Vinny a look down the table that Allie couldn't interpret.

"Where's the bread?" Vince asked. He was a growing boy —already big—and Allie figured he probably ate a lot.

"Oh, shoot," Loretta said. "I forgot it." She went to get up, but Vince stopped her.

"I'll get it, Nonna, since I'm the oldest." He stood.

"Actually, I'm the oldest," Gabe said. "I could get it."

"You don't even know where stuff is," Vince boomed.

Allie tensed. "Just let Vince get it, Gabe."

Gabe stood anyway. "It's bread. I think I can find it." He was never one to back down from an argument. Maybe he'd be a lawyer like his dad.

"I'm the oldest Marino," Vince snapped. "And a lot bigger than you."

Gabe's chest puffed out. "I'll be fourteen in three weeks, almost two years older."

They had a staredown, standing across the table from each other. She turned to Vinny, who lifted his hand like *wait and see*. All of the boys watched with interest.

Vince jerked his chin. "When's your birthday?"

"January thirtieth," Gabe returned.

"Ha! Mine's August thirteenth. More like a year and a half apart."

Gabe scowled. "You can't do math. It's six *and a half* months plus a year."

"Ooh, a big old half. Two weeks make you feel like a big man? Because you've got at least a foot to catch up to me."

"Do not!" Gabe barked.

"Come on," Vince challenged. "Back to back." He turned sideways.

All the boys looked over at Gabe to see if he'd take the height challenge.

"Both of you sit down," Vinny ordered. "I'll get the bread."

The boys sat. Vinny went to the kitchen.

"I'll get the punch," Vince said, standing again and glowering down at Gabe. "Dad bought it special for tonight."

"You just want to serve yourself first," Nico said.

"Shut it, Nico," Vince said, shoving the side of Nico's head. "I'll give it out fairly, split six ways." He stopped and turned to his grandmother. "Would you like some?"

Loretta waved the offer away and Vince turned to Allie. "Ms. Reynolds?"

"No, thank you," Allie said.

Vince took only his glass and left.

She turned to Gabe and told him to simmer down. "He started it," Gabe mumbled.

Vince returned with his glass filled and set it down.

"Bring the punch in here to pour," Loretta said.

Vince nodded once and left. Nico glanced over his shoulder, where Vince had just been, and then grinned before taking a gulp of punch from Vince's glass. He set it back and made a shushing noise at the boys.

By the time Vince got back, all the boys were snickering.

"What?" Vince barked.

Angel tattled. "Nico drank some of your punch."

Vince glared at Nico, who quickly denied it. The boys were all laughing now and not quietly.

Vince glared at all of them. "No respect."

Allie bit back a smile. That Vince was a firecracker. She really liked him.

After Vinny walked Allie and her kids back to their car, thanking them all for coming, he went back to Loretta's kitchen for the verdict. She was washing dishes.

"I'll get that, Loretta," he said. "You just take it easy. You made dinner."

She picked up her glass of red wine from the counter and surprised him by actually taking a seat at the square kitchen table. Normally she'd insist on doing the work or at least helping.

"You okay?" he asked.

"Come, take a seat."

This was the moment he'd been waiting for. Did she approve of Allie? And why did it matter so much to him? He supposed it was his way of hoping his moving forward was okay with Maria. He pulled out a seat. "I thought that went okay."

She took a sip of wine, saying nothing.

He waited her out, tense as all hell.

Finally she set her glass down. "Vinny, you keep up Sunday family dinner, even when the boys are full grown with families of their own. It'll keep them close, give them the continuity they need."

He smiled, shaking his head. That was so far away. They were kids!

She became stern, glaring at him. "Promise me, or I will haunt you beyond the grave."

Alarmed, he leaned close. "Come on, now, don't talk like that. You feeling okay?"

"Maria would've done the same," she said in a choked voice. "She knew the importance of Sunday family dinner."

"Okay, I promise. I'll keep up the tradition."

"I'm moving to Maryland."

It felt like she'd sucker punched him. He couldn't breathe for a moment. Loretta had been a rock for him and the kids through everything. It must be because of Allie. Loretta didn't want him moving on. What was he supposed to do, choose between his kids' grandmother and the woman he loved?

"Loretta, we still want you to be part of things."

"You don't need me."

"The kids do."

She shook her head. "Not like they used to."

He couldn't make this choice between two people who were so important to him. It wasn't fair.

He clenched his jaw. "Is this because of Allie?"

She patted his cheek. "You're a good man. And now that I've met Allie, I'm satisfied. I give you my blessing."

His jaw dropped.

She laughed. "Why so shocked?"

"Because you're leaving."

"It's for Rob. He had his first baby. A little girl." That was Maria's younger brother.

"Little Robbie?"

"Not so little anymore. He's been married five years now. He and his wife both work full time and asked me to move in with them. I'll still visit you, but I see now that you're in good hands with Allie."

"Loretta, I don't know what to say. This is all so sudden. Are you sure?"

She sighed. "I'm ready for a fresh start. This old house has so many memories, ghosts of a life that has long passed."

He could see that. This was the house Maria had been raised in. "I understand." He instantly felt lighter. "Your blessing means a lot to me, Loretta."

"She's a good woman. Did you see how she refused wine out of responsibility for her children?"

"You pushed her on that, testing her."

"Maybe. I can tell she's a good mom, a good woman." She gave him a watery smile. "Perhaps my grandchildren might have a mom to look after them."

His blood thrummed through his veins, all of his nerve endings electric and alive just at the thought of having Allie join his family. "She's a great woman."

"I see a long and happy future for you and Allie."

Joy rushed through him, everything in him ready for Allie, ready to love her, to bring her in close and keep her there. "Thank you, Loretta, for everything you've done for me and the boys. I couldn't have—"

"It's family," she said with a note of finality. "No thanks necessary."

"Thank you all the same. Anything you need anytime, you just call…" He got choked up.

She took his hand, kissed it and held it to her soft cheek. He bowed his head, closing his stinging eyes.

Vince's voice startled him. "Yo, Dad, can we stay a while longer? Angel and Jared screwed up the train set layout, and me and Nico wanna fix it."

"You boys stay as long as you like," Loretta said.

"Sure," Vinny told him. Their days at their Nonna's house were numbered.

"Thanks, Nonna! Thanks, Dad!" Vince turned, hollering, "Nico, Dad said okay! Angel, you watch and don't touch nothing."

When it was just the two of them again, Vinny asked, "When do you move?"

"In two weeks. I'll tell the boys when they're done with the train. I'll come back with Rob to get the house on the market in the spring. And, of course, I expect you to bring the boys to visit. It's not that far a drive."

"We will. Absolutely." He paused, thinking of the huge change for the boys. "They'll be upset."

"Maybe, for a short time, but I'll call. And you'll keep up Sunday family dinner. Maybe you'll soon add Allie's family to the tradition."

"I love her," he said.

"I know you do."

His throat was so tight with emotion he couldn't speak. Instead he stood, leaning down and kissing her cheek in gratitude. She smiled.

"I need to go see Allie," he said. "I hope to be back with good news."

Loretta tapped the kitchen table. "I'll be right here waiting to hear it."

Vinny dashed out the door, his kids occupied in the basement, and got into his car. He backed out of the driveway and forced himself to go the speed limit despite the urgent need he felt to get to Allie, to tell her everything right away. This was it. He knew it was right between them, and now that their kids got along as good as boys ever did at first meeting, he was sure it would be smooth sailing from here on out.

He made it to her place, pulled into the driveway, and strode up the front walk, nerves jangling. He went up the front porch, blew out a breath, and rang the bell.

She answered a moment later, looking impossibly beautiful, her blue eyes wide, her cheeks flushed. "Vinny! What're you doing here? Is everything okay?"

"Everything is great. Tonight told me everything I need to know. Allie, I love you. I never thought I'd love again, and I can't believe how lucky I am to have found you."

She gave him a soft smile, her gaze tender. "I love you too."

"I don't have a ring yet, but I'll get one." He went down on one knee. Her jaw dropped. "Allie, will you marry me?"

She stared at him.

"Allie?"

"Vinny, get up, please."

Shit. He rose to his feet. "You turning me down?"

She stared at the ground. "I need to think about it." She lifted her head, her eyes pained. "I only divorced four months ago."

"So that's a no."

"I'm just…this is so unexpected. I need to think about it, okay?"

His gut clenched. "I'll go."

She reached out and grabbed his arm. "Thank you for understanding."

He grunted, beyond nice words. "Night, Allie."

He turned and left, his limbs heavy. He'd gone for the touchdown pass and overthrew it by a mile.

10

Allie spent the whole week in a torturous tangle of emotions, alternately berating herself for turning down the love of her life and then knowing waiting was the right thing, feeling protective of her kids. After all, her boys had just met Vinny and then what? She was suddenly going to spring it on them that they were getting married?

And then she started thinking of what it would mean for her personally. Living with Vinny could be wonderful, but did they have what it took for the long haul? She didn't know. They'd only dated four months. And was she ready to be a mom to six boys? Holy hell! The chaos, the noise, the dirt, the looming teen years. She shuddered at the thought.

Friday morning she still didn't have any solid answers and felt incredibly guilty leaving Vinny hanging. She should just tell him definitively yes or no. No man wanted to wait around for an answer. She climbed the steps to her art studio, opened the door, and stopped short. An envelope addressed to her in Vinny's big confident scrawl lay at her feet. She grabbed it, heart racing, half afraid it was a breakup letter. She ripped it open and pulled out the folded note with shaking hands.

Allie,

This art studio reminds me of the beginning when we were just friends, and look at how far we've come since then. Not just us as a couple, on our own too. You a successful artist and me finally confident as a single dad, something I never thought I'd be. Maybe that'll change tomorrow. Ha! But right now we're both in a good place, and I'd like to be in that good place together. It's been three years. The kids can handle it.

I know we're meant to be together. I promise I will wait as long as it takes for that to happen.

Love,

Vinny

Tears stung her eyes. Here she was torturing herself over making a decision and he'd made it easy with a promise to wait for her. He was an honorable man, and she knew she could count on him to keep that promise. He wouldn't bail in light of her indecision. She took a deep breath for what felt like the first time in a week, all of the tension draining from her. The pressure was off. Maybe now they could go back to dating like before, slowly including the kids in more things. She hadn't spoken to Vinny all week, not knowing her answer. And he'd given her some space to think.

Had it really been three years they'd known each other? She thought back, it was close. Nearly three years since the day they'd met under very different circumstances. Three years of friendship, never knowing if they would ever have the right time to be together. They'd kept the connection, needing what each other offered—a light in the darkness.

~

Just as she'd hoped, things went back to normal with Vinny. They didn't speak of the proposal; he didn't press and she didn't bring it up. They dated. At her request, they had their usual Saturday night date and did something with all of the kids together on Sunday during the weekends she had them. Allie watched her boys carefully for signs of unhappiness, acting out, but they seemed to accept that some weekends they saw their dad and some weekends they hung out with Vinny and his kids. She hadn't heard any harrowing reports of them running wild in the city with their dad. Maybe things were settling down, or maybe winter in New York City was just too damn cold for them to want to escape their dad's apartment and run around. Her ex, surprisingly, was thrilled she had a serious boyfriend. Apparently, there was a clause in their divorce agreement that said if she remarried, he could stop paying alimony. He was all for her marrying Vinny, the sooner, the better because then he'd just have to pay child support. *Gee, thanks for your well wishes, William!*

As far as the six boys getting along, it helped immensely that Angel and Jared were both the youngest and most easygoing. The older boys focused on them whenever things became awkward, not knowing what to do with each other. All of the older boys were well used to looking out for their younger brothers. The boys got along more or less, as long as Vince didn't get his back up about Gabe being the oldest. Vinny's boys had really grown on her. She'd seen the sweetness in the older two, Vince and Nico, just below the surface, and Angel's sweetness was apparent in every beaming smile he gave her.

It was Sunday and everyone was at her house, the boys gathered in the living room playing video games. It was noisy, but happy noise. She and Vinny were in the kitchen, where he was preparing lasagna and she was enjoying watching him cook.

He put two trays of lasagna in the oven, set the timer, and turned to her. "I was waiting to get you alone."

"You were, huh? We'll have to be quick."

He chuckled and went to where he'd left his jacket on a hook by the back door, returning to her with an envelope. "Happy Valentine's Day, love."

Her heart squeezed. "I have your card too." She pulled it from the kitchen drawer and handed it to him, going up on tiptoe to kiss him. "Happy Valentine's Day. No one I'd rather spend it with."

"How much longer 'til we eat?" Vince hollered from the other room.

"An hour!" Vinny boomed.

"Can I have a snack?" Vince asked.

"No!" Vinny replied.

Silence.

Vinny smiled at her, his dark eyes twinkling with amusement. "Where were we with our romantic Valentine's Day with kids? Why did we include them in this again?"

"It's good for them to get to know each other."

"Okay, then." He jerked his chin. "Open it."

She opened her card. It was a funny one with a cartoonish dog on the front. She opened it to find a gift certificate for a massage.

He pointed at it. "I thought you might need one after all the time you spend with your kids and my kids too." He lifted one corner of his mouth. "The tension can really pile up. Anyway, if you like it, I'll arrange for you to go every month. I just want you to feel good, even though I know it's not easy with your kids and my kids."

She burst into tears.

"Oh, shit, don't cry." He pulled her close, pressing her head to his chest. "Never mind. You don't have to get a massage."

They were happy tears, but she couldn't stop crying long enough to explain. Vinny was worried about her being a mom to six boys, and wanted to take care of her. He experienced all the same tensions and never broke a sweat. An amazing man. He pulled his weight as a dad to his kids and had treated hers just like his own from day one.

He squeezed her tighter. "Allie, please stop crying. I feel terrible."

She lifted her head. "I'm happy."

His eyes widened. "You are?"

She wiped her tears from her cheeks and sniffled. "Happy tears." She pulled back from him and went down on her knees.

He stared at her. "Maybe we should, um, move somewhere more private."

She laughed. "Those were happy tears because I just now realized what a great husband you will be. A great partner. Vinny, will you marry me?"

"You're asking—yes!" He grabbed her, lifting her right off the ground and spinning her around, making her laugh. He set her on her feet and framed her face with his hands. "This is the best Valentine's gift I've ever gotten."

"Me too. You know why I fell so hard for you?"

His thumb stroked her cheek. "Why?"

"You have soul. I've never met a man so open and expressive."

He stilled. "That was Maria. She formed me. She was the one who was so open and expressive, and I tried to meet her halfway. I was still a kid when I fell for her, seventeen, and it changed me. She gave me that. I guess in a way she gave me you, since you like that about me."

"I *love* that about you." She paused, thinking of his first love. "Maria sounds like a very special woman."

He pressed his lips tightly together. "She was. Angel's a lot like her."

"Angel's a fantastic kid." Her throat tightened. "Vinny, I know I could never take her place. I would never try to for you or your boys."

"I don't see it like that, one person replacing another. It's more like, you and I, we're in a different place now. The *right* place for each other."

She hugged him tight and he wrapped his arms around her, surrounding her with warmth and love. He'd waited for her to be ready, for her boys to be ready, and welcomed her in with open arms.

A promise kept.

EPILOGUE

Two months later…

Allie couldn't help her beaming smile as Vinny waltzed with her during their pre-wedding ballroom dance lessons. It was only their first lesson, but he'd picked up the box step quickly.

He pulled her in close, leaning down to whisper in her ear, "Tell me again why the boys are taking dance lessons with us."

She smiled serenely. "So they can bond."

"They're making faces at each other."

She glanced over at Vince, dancing with a woman with curly gray hair in her fifties. Vince's eyes were crossed. Gabe and Luke were snickering. Then Luke made a snarly face back.

Their class had three other couples and a group of five middle-aged women from a divorce support group. Allie felt a little bad about the numbers here. Surely, the divorced women had hoped to meet single men, just not men quite so young. So far, the boys had refused to dance with each other.

She looked up at Vinny. "They're bonded in their dislike of waltzing. And look at how well Gabe's doing with his partner."

Gabe looked a little stiff, but he was definitely doing the correct box step with his divorcée, a blond woman who kept looking around, maybe hoping for another man to magically appear instead of a teenaged boy.

"Yeah, well," Vinny said, looking a little guilty.

"What?"

He lowered his voice. "I paid Gabe to set an example for the other boys."

"What!"

"They were plotting to revolt. I had to do something."

She bit back a smile. That was just wrong. On the other hand, Vinny knew how much this meant to her and had smoothed the way. "What if the others find out?"

He arched a brow. "Payment is contingent on keeping his mouth shut. Besides, he's the oldest. He should set an example." He gave Gabe a thumbs-up, and Gabe acknowledged it with a subtle head nod.

Vinny gazed down at her tenderly, his hand leaving her waist to slide up her back and stroke her hair. "They're good kids, but ya can't blame boys for not being into ballroom dance. And six weeks of lessons is a *lot* at that age."

She laughed. "Their wives will thank me one day."

He smiled, his dark eyes crinkling at the corners. "Maybe so."

Luke passed by with his divorcée.

"Nice footwork," Vinny commented to Luke. "How do we look?"

Luke took in her and Vinny before finally saying coolly, "Fine."

Vinny inclined his head. "I'll take fine." He moved them a distance away, a little more subdued.

"He'll warm up," Allie said. "Just give him time."

"No rush," Vinny said.

"He's stubborn is all," Allie said. "It's not personal."

Luke had stewed after they'd announced their engagement, keeping his concerns to himself until just last week before Sunday dinner when he'd surprised her by confronting

Vinny, who was preparing ravioli in the kitchen. She'd been making the salad.

Luke, all of ten years old, had crossed his arms and informed Vinny in a belligerent tone, "You're not my real dad and you never will be."

"Luke!" she'd exclaimed, shocked he'd speak like that to Vinny, who'd just been innocently cooking dinner.

Vinny held up a staying hand to her, but kept his gaze on Luke. "I know that, but you know what? Me getting to be your stepdad, that's a gift for me. And I promise to treat you like one of my own."

Luke's arms uncrossed, and he looked uncertain, like maybe he wanted to believe Vinny, but he wasn't so sure.

"You like baseball?" Vinny asked.

Luke jerked his chin. "Yeah."

"Tell the guys after dinner we'll play a game. We're lucky to have you and your brothers in the mix. Now we can finally have a real game."

Luke bolted, shouting, "Guys! We're playing ball after dinner!"

It was a start. She was sure Luke and Vinny would connect soon. It was impossible not to with Vinny being such a great dad.

She squeaked as Vinny got fancy with his newfound dance moves, spinning her around and then back.

"Look at you with all the moves," she teased.

He looked over her shoulder. "Jared just made a break for it."

"What!"

"I'll get him."

He left and returned a few moments later, one big hand on the back of Jared's neck, marching him back in. Jared was grinning, saying, "I was just getting a drink!"

Jared adored Vinny because Vinny had been teaching him to work with tools. Jared was quite mechanically gifted, something she wouldn't have known without Vinny in their lives.

A moment later, Jared pulled Angel away from the

instructor, an older woman with dyed black hair and a graceful dancer's body, and started dancing with him. The two boys stood, hands on each other's shoulders, a foot apart, talking the whole time.

Vinny swooped her up in his arms and spun her around, making her laugh. He set her back on her feet and resumed the slow box step. "I told Jared it was either Angel or Miss Beasley. He picked Angel."

"See? They're bonding."

The boys—all six of them—grimaced and snickered their way through class, which was fine by her, as long as they were learning.

They all walked out together after class, the boys quiet for once. Then Vinny announced, "You boys did such a great job, let's stop for ice cream on the way home."

The boys erupted in cheers.

Vinny smiled at her and winked. She smiled back.

And then the best part—the whole ride to the ice-cream place the boys noisily talked about their "lame" dance lessons and who had the worst partner. Even Gabe and Vince shared a good laugh. Which was exactly what she'd wanted.

Let the bonding begin!

~

Present day…

It was Valentine's Day, always a special time for her and Vinny since it was their engagement anniversary. They were at the Clover Park Valentine's Day dance, all dressed up and feeling romantic. They'd been surprised upon arrival to find their six sons in attendance with their wives and kids. Guess they wanted to start their own Valentine's Day tradition here too. Now she and Vinny had the dance floor all to themselves because Angel had requested a special dance just for them. Such a sweetheart.

Vinny took the lead in a waltz, surprisingly graceful for a man of his size. She silently congratulated herself on getting him to take ballroom dance lessons before their wedding. It had paid off in spades, giving her years of wonderful dancing with him for special occasions or just when the mood struck in their kitchen.

As soon as the dance ended, the band quieted, so she and Vinny left the dance floor. Angel ran up to the microphone, holding a black leather-bound book, and she suddenly knew what was going on. He was honoring them as a couple because she and Vinny had been there for the not-so-easy paths to the altar of Angel and Julia and all of their children.

Angel's voice rang out to the crowded room. "Attention, everyone, thanks for giving me a moment to acknowledge two very special people celebrating their anniversary today, Vinny and Allie Marino."

Everyone applauded. Allie flushed and exchanged a look with Vinny. It was their engagement anniversary. When Angel had mentioned making a keepsake book before, she'd thought he'd meant for their wedding anniversary in June.

"Anniversary of their engagement," Angel added. "We wanted to surprise them with an early gift and a toast. To the two people whose love brought all of us together." He gestured over to his brothers and their wives. "Six boys in one house, you can imagine the chaos."

Her sons grinned. The crowd tittered.

Vinny cupped his hands around his mouth, hollering, "Allie kept you boys in line!"

Allie smacked his arm playfully. "Vinny!"

Angel smiled. "She did. Always with an open heart. We all love you very much, Ma."

Tears sprang to her eyes. Angel, being the youngest, had needed her most. She rushed on stage and hugged him. Vinny followed a moment later, standing by her side.

Angel cleared his throat and continued. "If there's one thing we learned bringing two families together, it's—" He gestured over to his brothers to join in. They all droned in unison: "Love doesn't divide, it multiplies!"

She and Vinny laughed. That had been their mantra in the early years.

Vinny leaned toward the microphone. "Finally, they learned!" He shook his finger at their sons.

She beamed, knowing her part in achieving family harmony. Her popular picture book series, The Huddle-Cuddles, featuring her sons as hedgehogs and her stepsons as porcupines, had taught them lessons on working out their differences through a series of adventures.

Angel went on. "So corny and so true. It was what our parents said when we'd argue over who had the real mom or the real dad. Now we all know how much they both love us. The best mom and dad any of us could ask for." He handed her the keepsake book and spoke away from the microphone. "This is from all of us. It starts at your wedding since that's when we had the most pictures."

The cover had a rectangular opening for a picture, and he'd put in the wedding picture with all of them in it. The young boys all lined up, a contrast in looks, dark-haired dark-eyed Italian kids next to her fair-haired, light-skinned kids. They were all smiling, but only Angel and Jared were beaming, eight years old and thrilled to have each other. The picture perfectly encapsulated where their family was at back then, just beginning to bond. And they'd made it work.

"We love all of you!" Allie exclaimed, taking them all in. "I can't wait to pore over this at home tonight. Now get out there and dance! Ladies, make them show you their ballroom dance moves! You better believe I made every one of them take lessons." *You're welcome, ladies.*

Her daughters-in-law laughed and did as told, guiding their husbands on the dance floor. Angel stepped away from the microphone and went to Julia. The band started playing again with no singer this time because the lead singer was Gabe's wife, and she flew off stage and into his arms.

Everyone started dancing again.

Vinny took her hand and led her back to the dance floor. As they passed each son with his wife, they thanked them. Gabe's loving smile meant a lot to her because the one letter he'd read had been from Vinny, saying "It's been three years. The kids can handle it." The letter wasn't dated. Without knowing the journey she and Vinny had travelled, it might have sounded like a scandalous affair. She and Vinny had chosen not to explain themselves, both because it was private and because they hoped Gabe and all of their children knew them well enough to know they respected the marriage vows too much to ever sully them. Their shining example of a loving marriage seemed to have the right effect. All of their sons were happily married.

They reached Angel and Julia, who'd gone to so much trouble to make tonight special, and thanked them profusely.

Vinny winked at Angel. "Maybe one day your kids will want to hear your story."

"Not much to tell," Angel returned with a wink. "We met, we dated, we got married, end of story." Those had been Vinny's words. Angel and Julia's journey to marriage had been twisty with loads of complications. It had all worked out in the end.

Allie smiled and squeezed Angel's arm before Vinny whisked her off.

Some things were too romantic to share with the world. Especially your kids!

Dear readers, I hope you enjoyed seeing how it all began with Vinny and Allie. Now it's time for crazy Gran O'Hare's love story with her beloved Patrick back when they were both so young (yet legal age LOL). Don't miss *Maggie Meets Her Match*!

Maggie Meets Her Match

Good girl Maggie Murphy is trapped in a conventional life not of her choosing, so when she meets bad boy Patrick O'Hare, she thinks she might've just found the man to spring her free. By ruining her.

Patrick O'Hare is stuck. He flubbed the tryouts that would've made him a pro football player, and now he's spending the summer working for his uncle's traveling carnival company and trying to figure out who he is without football.

Sizzling summer nights soon lead to a future neither of them could have imagined. But can two very different people follow their dreams together?

Sign up for my newsletter and never miss a new release! https://www.kyliegilmore.com/newsletter

ALSO BY KYLIE GILMORE

Unleashed Romance <<steamy romcoms with dogs!

Fetching (Book 1)

Dashing (Book 2)

Sporting (Book 3)

Toying (Book 4)

Blazing (Book 5)

Chasing (Book 6)

Daring (Book 7)

Leading (Book 8)

Racing (Book 9)

Loving (Book 10)

The Clover Park Series <<brothers who put family first!

The Opposite of Wild (Book 1)

Daisy Does It All (Book 2)

Bad Taste in Men (Book 3)

Kissing Santa (Book 4)

Restless Harmony (Book 5)

Not My Romeo (Book 6)

Rev Me Up (Book 7)

An Ambitious Engagement (Book 8)

Clutch Player (Book 9)

A Tempting Friendship (Book 10)

Clover Park Bride: Nico and Lily's Wedding

A Valentine's Day Gift (Book 11)

Maggie Meets Her Match (Book 12)

The Clover Park Charmers series <<sweet and sexy charmers!

Almost Over It (Book 1)

Almost Married (Book 2)

Almost Fate (Book 3)

Almost in Love (Book 4)

Almost Romance (Book 5)

Almost Hitched (Book 6)

Happy Endings Book Club Series <<the Campbell family and a romance book club collide!

Hidden Hollywood (Book 1)

Inviting Trouble (Book 2)

So Revealing (Book 3)

Formal Arrangement (Book 4)

Bad Boy Done Wrong (Book 5)

Mess With Me (Book 6)

Resisting Fate (Book 7)

Chance of Romance (Book 8)

Wicked Flirt (Book 9)

An Inconvenient Plan (Book 10)

A Happy Endings Wedding (Book 11)

The Rourkes Series <<swoonworthy princes and kickass princesses!

Royal Catch (Book 1)

Royal Hottie (Book 2)

Royal Darling (Book 3)

Royal Charmer (Book 4)

Royal Player (Book 5)

Royal Shark (Book 6)

Rogue Prince (Book 7)

Rogue Gentleman (Book 8)

Rogue Rascal (Book 9)

Rogue Angel (Book 10)

Rogue Devil (Book 11)

Rogue Beast (Book 12)

**Check out my website for the most up-to-date list of my books:
kyliegilmore.com/books**

ABOUT THE AUTHOR

Kylie Gilmore is the *USA Today* bestselling author of over fifty humorous contemporary romances. Her series include Unleashed Romance, the Rourkes, the Happy Endings Book Club, Clover Park, and Clover Park Charmers. With more than three million downloads of her books, readers all over the world love escaping into her hilarious feel-good romances featuring strong bonds with family, friends, and community.

Kylie lives in New York with her family, a demanding cat, and a nutso dog. When she's not writing, reading hot romance, or dutifully taking notes at writing conferences, you can find her flexing her muscles all the way to the high cabinet for her secret chocolate stash.

Sign up for Kylie's Newsletter and get a FREE book! kyliegilmore.com/newsletter

For text alerts on Kylie's new releases, text KYLIE to the number (888) 707-3025. (US only)

For more fun stuff check out Kylie's website https://www.kyliegilmore.com.

Thanks for reading *A Valentine's Day Gift*. I hope you enjoyed it. Would you like to know about new releases? You can sign up for my new release email list at https://www.kyliegilmore.com/newsletter. I promise not to clog your inbox! Only new release info, sales, and some fun giveaways.

I love to hear from readers! You can find me at:
kyliegilmore.com
Instagram.com/kyliegilmore
Facebook.com/KylieGilmoreToo
Twitter @KylieGilmoreToo

If you liked Vinny and Allie's story, please leave a review on your favorite retailer's website or Goodreads. Thank you.